MW00440666

Damnation

Book 1
Blue Moon Saloon

by Anna Lowe

TWIN MOON PRESS

Contents

Other books in this series

Damnation (Book 1)

Temptation (Book 2)

Redemption (Book 3)

Salvation (Book 4)

Perfection (a short story prequel to the series)

visit www.annalowebooks.com

Free Books

Get your free e-books now!

Sign up for my newsletter at *annalowebooks.com* to get three free books!

- *Desert Wolf: Friend or Foe* (Book 1.1 in the Twin Moon Ranch series)

- *Off the Charts* (the prequel to the Serendipity Adventure series)

- *Perfection* (the prequel to the Blue Moon Saloon series)

Chapter One

"Are you sure you want to do this?" Tina asked.

Jessica forced herself to keep up a steady, confident stride and nodded firmly. "I want to do this."

I need to do this was more like it, but pride was about the only thing she had left.

Tina glanced at her, but Jessica kept walking down the sidewalk in the dusty western town, pretending not to notice. She was getting to be a champ at pretending lots of things, like the fact she wasn't shaking inside.

Run! Run away! her inner wolf screamed.

If she hadn't had her sister, Janna, to think of, Jessica might have done just that — hit the road running and never looked back. Except she'd tried that already, and it hadn't worked.

Time to stop running, she told her inner wolf.

We don't know this pack. We don't know this place, her wolf whined.

"This is going to be great!" Janna smiled. "Is that the saloon?"

Janna wasn't just putting on a brave face. She actually was excited about what she'd called their lucky break. As if they were lucky to have lost their pack to a band of rogues one awful night six months ago. As if they

1

were lucky to be leapfrogging from one place to another in search of some safe refuge.

Jess shook her head. God, she was getting bitter. Her sister was right. This could be their lucky break. They'd found a pack willing to set them up with work and a place to stay. And not just any pack, but Twin Moon, one of the most powerful packs to emerge in the Southwest in recent years. Tina Hawthorne-Rivera was a leading member of that pack, and she seemed to have a soft spot for wayward shifters in need of a second chance.

Jessica bit her lip, thinking about the long road she'd traveled in the past few months. Maybe she and Janna could finally stop looking over their shoulders and catch their breath.

"That's the place," Tina replied, waving to the two-story building owned by her pack. "Blue Moon Saloon."

Jess drew in a long breath and slowed to look it over.

She couldn't have conjured anything more *Wild West* out of her imagination if she'd tried. The whole historic center of the old town was like that — a high-altitude frontier town, barely dragged into modern times.

"Perfect location, just a block off Whiskey Row." Tina nodded in pride.

Jessica's inner wolf whined. *I like home better.*

Yes, well, home was gone, and she could never go back to that place.

Want my mate, the wolf whimpered.

Yeah, well. *He didn't want us.* When would the stupid beast get that through its head?

Anger worked better than the grief that welled up every time she thought of that part of her past, so she hung on to it for the time being. She combed her long, brown hair back and stood at her full five foot eight. She needed this job, damn it. She'd get it.

"This is so cute!" Janna exclaimed. "Don't you think, Jess?"

She took in the peeling paint, the dusty windows. *Cute* might describe the empty shop to the right, but not the saloon, which was dark and dreary, just like the people who gravitated toward a place like that, she'd bet. Waitressing, she didn't mind. But getting her ass pinched... No, thanks.

She glanced at her reflection in the glass and grimaced at her worn jeans and checkered top. Maybe she didn't have to worry about getting harassed. She'd gone from lean and athletic to downright gaunt in the past couple of months.

"The saloon ran well for years — well enough to pay the rent, at least — but the man we were leasing it to retired, and the new guys only took it over a month ago."

Jess raised an eyebrow in a question.

Tina gave a tiny nod and lowered her voice. "Shifters, like us. None of the neighbors know." Her stern look made it clear that none of the neighbors could ever find out. That was a given in the shifter world. The constant secrecy, the veil of normalcy. Shifters could blend in perfectly as long as they kept their beast sides tightly leashed.

Tina tilted her head toward the wooded hills surrounding the town. "Good place to run when you need a break."

When your wolf needs a break, she meant. Every shifter needed a chance to let their inner animals run free — and not only under the light of a full moon.

3

"The building is over a hundred years old," Tina went on, speaking louder again.

Yes, she could see it in the detailed moldings, the ornate windows, the false front.

"The ground floor is really three units, but two were combined for the saloon."

Jessica's eyes kept traveling to the smaller place on the right. The cute one. "What's in there?"

Tina sighed. "It used to be a small art gallery. Before that, a café. But we haven't been able to find a renter for it in years."

God, if she had some start-up capital... Jessica shook the thought off. It would take a hell of a lot of tips to get to the point where she could even think about that. And until she had peace of mind about the rogues hounding her... Why even wish?

"You can live upstairs," Tina said. "If you're sure you don't want to stay on the ranch. We do have the space, you know."

Jess wasn't sure about anything, but living among a pack of strangers didn't really appeal. Not even a whole pack of wolves as nice as Tina. Plus, neither Jess nor Janna had their own wheels, and even if they did, the forty-five-minute commute into town each day — and each late night — would be a bit much.

"This will be fine," Jess said, trying to keep doubt out of her voice.

"It will need some work..." Tina warned.

Jessica wondered if she meant the saloon, the apartment upstairs, or the whole new life she faced now.

"...and you'll have to share a bathroom with the guys..."

"No problem!" Janna chirped.

4

God, Jessica hoped not. That was the other unknown in the equation. She'd have to live under the same roof as her new boss or bosses. Who were the two men running the place, anyway? Shifters, was all she knew.

"They're good guys," Tina added quickly. "Hard-working. Honest."

She sure hoped so.

"...a little rough around the edges, maybe..."

Jess pictured natty beards, worn jeans, western drawls.

"...but I'm sure they'll be fine. And they can really use your help."

That was another thing. Everything Tina *didn't* say suggested the saloon wasn't exactly off to a stellar start. Not that Jess minded hard work, but it would be nice to be part of a successful, competent team.

"Anything you need, you let me know," Tina said.

"Thanks," Jess said, meeting her eyes so Tina knew she meant it. The she-wolf had gone out of her way to help Jess and Janna from the very start.

She's got a soft spot for outcasts, Tina's mate, Rick, had explained back on the ranch, when he'd looked at Tina like she was the sun and he was the moon, devoted to orbiting faithfully to the end of his days.

The saloon doors — a pair of real saloon doors that swung both ways — split open, and a tall figure strode out.

"Hello, Ty," Tina said while Jessica and Janna hung back.

Tina was probably the only person west of the Missouri who could greet that man so casually. Jessica's eyes hit the ground, and not just because it was a required sign of submission to the alpha of Twin Moon pack. The man

5

had a pointed, laser glare, and sheer wolf power sloughed off him in waves.

"Hi," he growled.

Once upon a time, Jess had made a habit of showing such men she wasn't easily impressed, but she'd been on the run long enough to know to keep her place. Just in case.

"Don't mind my brother," Tina whispered out of the corner of her mouth, then swept right by him and into the saloon.

Ty Hawthorne held the left half of the saloon door open in a surprisingly polite gesture for an alpha that powerful, and for a moment, the *watch-your-step-on-my-turf* aura he gave off softened to a more gentle, *you'll-be-safe-here*.

Jess took a last, deep breath and walked through the doors, feeling as if she were leaping into a deep, murky pool.

At first, she couldn't see anything, but as her eyes adjusted to the dim interior, she could make out the trappings of an authentic saloon. Four poker tables stood in the middle, and booths lined the sides. A weathered sign on the right read, *Check your guns at the door*, and it was hard to tell whether the message was a gag or not. Otherwise, the walls were decorated with black-and-white scenes of the frontier town in days gone by — all covered with enough dust to suggest that the new management hadn't changed the decor. Or the menu, judging by the faded chicken-scratch on the chalkboard by the front door. Not a soul in sight, but then, it was ten in the morning — before opening time.

Janna, of course, waltzed right in. "Great! A pool table."

There was a dartboard, too, a standup piano, and an old jukebox to one side. But the centerpiece of the saloon, and the thing that had Jess halt dead in her tracks, was the bar itself. A huge, oak masterpiece that took up all of the back wall. Bottles of booze glittered in the light bouncing off the huge mirror in the middle section, and an antique Winchester hung over the top. But it was the woodwork that caught her eye. Intricately carved wooden supports held up each of the many shelves, and a mountain scene was etched into the upper panel. A wolf howled at the moon, a bear waded in a stream, and an eagle soared overhead.

"Gorgeous," she murmured.

A finely crafted latticework covered the entire upper section, all the way to the molded tin ceiling of the room. The bar itself was polished to a glow in the sunlight filtering through the windows, as was the brass footrail underneath.

Two things were immediately evident. First, someone had put a hell of a lot of time into carving that bar a long, long time ago. Second, someone very recently had put a hell of a lot of time into restoring it all.

"Nice, huh?" Tina murmured.

"More than nice. It's spectacular," she agreed.

"My great-uncle made it, ninety years ago."

Pool balls clicked behind them, and Jessica spun to see her sister blow at the tip of a pool stick like a gunslinger who'd just made the perfect shot. Knowing Janna, it *was* a perfect shot. But didn't they have more important things to do, like meeting their new boss?

Jessica looked around. Spider webs filled the other corners of the place, but damn did that bar gleam. If the guy put as much work into the rest of the place as he had into the bar, it wouldn't be half bad. But the tables were crooked, the chairs chipped. The saloon had seen more than one brawl in its time. She was sure of that.

"Hello?" Tina called. Her voice echoed down a narrow hallway that appeared to lead to the kitchen and a back room.

"Coming," a deep voice came from out of sight.

Jessica's wolf perked its ears. Froze. Practically pointed like a goddamn hunting dog, too. She gave it a mental swat, but the beast didn't budge. What the hell was that about?

Her nostrils flared, but all she could pick up was the scent of the shifters around her and the stale smell of French fries.

"Be right there," a second voice came. A low, rumbly voice, like that of a bear roused from his den.

Her wolf soul had been slumbering for most of the morning, but now, it jumped up and down, growling at the bars of its cage. Wagging its tail frantically from a crazy cocktail of mixed emotions. Excitement with a splash of hope, a touch of arousal, and a whole lot of fear, clinking around like a couple of ice cubes in a whiskey glass.

What? She wanted to scream at her wolf. *What?*

Two square-shouldered forms stepped out of the shadows of the hallway, one half a step ahead of the other. Big, burly men who moved like bulldozers, confident that any living thing would back the hell out of their way. Each slowed to brush a shoulder against the doorframe as he came through, the way some shifters did to mark their turf.

Short, sandy hair. Scruffy stubble. Dark, wary eyes. Huge, steely hands clenched into fists. Two men who couldn't be anything but brothers.

A warm rush of adrenaline exploded inside her and bounced around her veins, and her mind whirled. *Not possible. It couldn't be. . .*

Part of her wanted to flee; the other part wanted to leap into an embrace. The man in front looked permanently stern, while the one behind smiled. At least, he did until he spotted her.

"Jessica Macks," Tina started the introductions, "meet—"

"Simon," Jess blurted, looking over the shoulder of the first man toward the second. "Voss," she finished, going weak in the knees.

The man she'd never stopped loving, no matter how hard she tried. The bear shifter who still inhabited all of her dreams.

Mate! Her wolf whimpered in joy. *Mate!*

Blue eyes the color of the coldest, clearest alpine lake locked on hers and refused to let go.

"Jessica," he murmured, too low for human ears.

Her wolf did a crazy tap dance. *Mate! Mine!*

"Wow!" Janna exclaimed, clueless as ever. "Simon?" Then she turned to the older brother — the one who was bigger, broader, and burlier, but only by a hair. "Soren? Oh my God! It really is you."

"Good to see you," Soren mumbled as his eyes darted between Jess and Simon.

"This is amazing!" Janna declared.

Tina tipped her head sideways in a gesture that said, *This is unexpected.*

Jessica shook her head furiously, trying to break Simon's unwavering gaze. *This is not possible.* No way. No how. The man who'd pretended to love her, then cast her aside?

"This..." Simon uttered in his deep, edgy bass. A sound like a shovel scraping against rock, guaranteed to send tingles to every fenced-off corner of her body and mind. "This will never work."

Jess edged toward the doorway, trying to keep the wobbling pieces of her heart together long enough to make her escape.

She shook her head and echoed him, trying to convince her wolf. "This will never work."

Chapter Two

For a split second, Simon stood stock-still, gaping while his inner bear reared up on its hind legs and roared.

Jessica. Jess. *His* Jess. Alive!

He wanted to drop to his knees and wrap himself around her legs. Wanted to crumple to the floor and cry in relief to see her alive. He wanted to roar to heaven that he finally, finally, had that second chance he'd been praying for, that all his hoping and wishing and dreaming hadn't been in vain.

But fuck. All he could get out were a few emotionless words. Why, why, why?

He couldn't think straight, that was why. Not upon seeing Jess alive but so haunted. The nervous tic in her cheek said she really, really needed the job. The full lips wobbled in fear and broken hope. The hollows around her incredible gray-blue eyes spoke of sleepless nights. Deep, dark wolf eyes that said she hadn't forgotten. Hadn't forgiven.

And why the hell should she?

"This will never work," he'd blurted, even as his bear roared. *No! No! No!*

Worse, Jess had immediately agreed. "This will never work." She even recoiled as she said it, putting another crack in his heart.

No. There was no way Jessica Macks could be back in his life.

The rear door to the alley was open, and he could hear the voice of fate drifting in from the desert. Laughing at him. Again.

Christ, how could he not have sensed that she was alive? That she was so near?

The whole conversation he'd had with Tina two days ago echoed in his mind, and it all seemed so obvious now.

"Good news! I think I found the help you need," Tina had said.

"Yeah? That would be great." The saloon needed all the help it could get. He and Soren had done their best, but they weren't exactly off to a good start.

"I came across two women — shifters — looking for a job and a place to stay."

He'd just nodded along, not thinking for one second Tina meant two she-wolves from Black River — the pack that had been neighbors with his clan back in Montana. Back before *it* happened. The *it* that he and Soren couldn't bear talking about, even if they thought about it all the time.

"Now, look, they're a little shy," Tina warned him.

That had caught him off guard. "What are we going to do with shy waitresses?"

"Well, only one of them is on the shy side."

Never in a million years would he ever have called his Jess shy. No wonder he hadn't suspected.

"And they both need a chance," Tina had said.

That, he could relate to. He and Soren had been badly in need of a chance, and Tina had given it to them. She'd talked the ruling alpha of the local wolf pack into letting the bear brothers revive an out-of-business saloon the pack owned in town. The least he could do was give someone else a chance, right?

"Where'd you say they come from?" he'd asked.

Tina answered vaguely. "Better not ask too many questions. Will you give them a chance? Please?"

So of course he'd said yes and yelled for confirmation from Soren, who nodded right along. Their previous waitress had lasted all of two days before she quit, and they couldn't run the place on their own.

But Jesus, he never suspected it would be *them*.

Lean and lanky like any good timber wolves, but tired, too. Jessica looked as proud and fierce as ever but much too worried and much too thin. Janna still had her trademark smile and sass. A couple of capable Montana girls, unafraid of getting their hands dirty or speaking their minds. And the second Jessica's gray-blue eyes hardened on him, his heart clenched.

This will never work. Had he really said that before fleeing to the back room?

Not like his brother had been any help with his flat, unimpressed greeting. "Good to see you."

Good to see you? His bear raged inside. *Just good?*

His stomach was doing flip-flops, his blood rushing in uneven bursts. His heart pounded halfway out of his chest. Good to fucking seeing you?

It wasn't just good to see Jess again. It was great. Overwhelming. Amazing.

He slumped to a chair in the back room and held his head in his hands. The only thing keeping him from dropping to his knees — even in the back room, even a minute after the shock — was the fact that the walls were too damn thin to cover the anguished noises he was likely to make if he let go the slightest, teensiest bit. So no knees. No noises. Just a hanging head and clenched fists and raspy breathing. The fervent wish that he'd died six months ago with the rest of his family. Better yet, that he'd died honorably, defending his mate. Because the life he'd been living the last six months wasn't living. It was existing, nothing more. And now that he'd seen Jessica alive and angry as ever, that existence was just as bleak.

Footsteps carried through the floorboards under the threadbare carpet, and Simon glanced up. His brother entered and leaned against the small bar built into the back room — the one they used for special occasions, or would, if they ever got enough business for something like that. Soren kept his distance and his hands out of his pockets, just in case. Which was good, because Simon was all too ready to lash out at the nearest punching bag, even if that was his own flesh and blood.

Soren looked him up and down for a full minute before opening his mouth. "Want to tell me what that was about?"

"No," he barked and dropped his head again.

"Fine," Soren growled. "Then let me tell you. We need the help. And what the Twin Moon wolves say, we do."

God, how low had he and his brother fallen that they were beholden to a pack of wolves?

"We have to," Soren said in a voice raspy with regret. "Just swallow whatever pride you have left and do what you have to do."

Do what you have to do. That line had been their mantra in the weeks following the annihilation of their clan. They'd come home three days too late to do anything but extinguish the last burning embers of what had once been home, then spent the next weeks hunting down the rogues responsible for the massacre. Or as many of the rogues as they could track down, because the murderers had splintered into smaller groups and parted ways.

Do what you have to do. It pushed them through the killing spree of their revenge, then teased them as they wandered aimlessly afterward, not sure where to go, what to do.

But there were some things he just couldn't do. Like live side by side with the woman he'd made sure would never, ever give him another chance.

"Don't," he growled at his brother. At his bear, too, because the damn beast was huffing and puffing and clawing him from the inside.

Soren pushed away from the bar and loomed over him. "Don't tell me don't."

It shouldn't have been enough to push him over the edge, but it was. Simon jumped to his feet and shoved his brother. Claws ripped out of his fingertips. His teeth pushed at his gums and his bear roared in fury inside. Who cared where he directed his anger? He couldn't fight fate, so the next best thing was his brother, right?

His brother, the only person in the world he had left.

Soren's eyes were dark and dangerous. Maybe Simon wasn't the only one who needed to punch his frustration out.

"Push me, little cub." Soren taunted him the way he'd done when they were kids, though his words hadn't had that murderous edge way back then.

"Watch what you wish for," he snapped right back.

They circled each other, ready to fight.

"You watch what you wish for—"

"Ahem."

15

Both their heads snapped around at the sound of Tina, clearing her throat from two steps away. Calm, collected, kindhearted Tina Hawthorne. Christ, what other woman in a five-hundred-mile radius had the balls to break up a bear brawl? Besides maybe Jess...

And just like that, the anger turned to shame. He dropped his eyes and forced the bristling hair on his neck to recede before any more of his bear got out.

Soren shot him a *this is your fault, asshole* look, and he was right. This was Tina, and they owed her, big-time. They owed Twin Moon pack, too, for giving them a chance.

Simon glanced up to apologize to Tina, and...shit. Her brother, Ty, the pack alpha, stood behind her looking *this* close to shifting into wolf form and joining the fray. If it had just been Ty, Simon might just have fought on, regardless of the consequences. But Tina — one little noise, and the room settled down. Sometimes, Simon had to wonder which sex was the more powerful one.

"I don't know what this is about," Tina started. "But I'm asking you—"

Ty's murderous glare said, *And I'm telling you—*

"—to help them out. To give them a chance."

She didn't say, *the same chance we gave you*, but it was written in the stern lines of her brow.

"Sure." Soren nodded quickly. "We're happy to give them a chance."

Ty socked Simon with a look that said, *I'm waiting.*

He held back from baring his teeth at the Twin Moon pack alpha, but only just. Hell, if he'd been born into Ty's position, he'd be the one glaring the wolf down. Except that's not the way it was. He was just a bear from a tiny northern clan that had been bled right out of exis-

16

tence. A bear who'd failed to protect his family when it counted most. A bear who should have died the minute his rampage of revenge was over because he had nothing to live for any more. A failure of a bear who...

He closed his eyes. A bear who owed these wolves for letting him settle on the outer fringe of their turf. He glanced up at Ty. Who could begrudge a good alpha for looking after his pack?

He could curse him, though, if under his breath. Goddamn wolves.

The words Simon forced out a second later, though, were resigned. "Sure. We'll give them a chance."

The alpha wolf glared a second longer, then nodded. "You will."

Chapter Three

"What's wrong?"

Jessica glanced from her own weary reflection in the bar mirror to that of her sister. God, how could Janna look so peppy at a time like this?

"Everything is wrong," she mumbled and let her shoulders droop. She was *this* close to rolling into a fetal position on the floor and giving up. But her stubborn-hearted wolf kept her on her feet.

We can do this! We can get our mate back!

If she wanted him back, which she didn't. And if he loved her, which he didn't. He'd made that absolutely clear.

"Jess, Simon is here. That's a good thing."

She shook her head, wishing she'd never told her younger sister about the fling she'd had all those years ago. How deeply she'd fallen in love with the sweetest, studliest bear. How badly he'd broken her heart.

"A good thing? Not so sure," she said.

Liar, her wolf scolded.

"Of course it's a good thing." Janna's hands swept around the saloon. "And look — we've got jobs in this great place."

Jessica let her gaze travel the room, stopping point-edly at the paint peeling off the window frames, the scrape marks on the floor, the rickety chairs that might or might not support a customer after a hearty meal.

"If we have jobs," she mumbled.

"Oh, come on," Janna said. "You've got to believe."

Easy for her kid sister to say, even if the twenty-seven-year-old was no longer a kid. She hadn't found her destined mate, only to have him laugh in her face.

A cold shudder came over her, and her thoughts jumped to the chance meeting in a blizzard that had started it all. A long time ago, before their packs even considered the idea of a closer alliance. She'd been forced to take refuge in a cave, and Simon had come lumbering in. In bear form, no less, scaring the bejesus out of her wolf, although all she had showed was a row of bared teeth. But one thing had led to another once they'd agreed to... um... keep each other warm, and she'd practically been floating when she left the cave two days later with a promise to see him again soon. It was as if destiny had swirled into that cave along with the most determined flakes of wind-driven snow and whispered in her ear. *He's the one. He's the one.*

They spent a whole year stealing off to clandestine trysts by the creek or behind the mills that lay where their territories intersected. A whole year of subtly convincing their families that a bear-wolf pairing would be a good thing. And she'd done it — she'd finally done it! She'd never forget her parents calling her in with the news.

"The bears have agreed to your betrothal to the Voss boy."

She'd hugged them both and danced around the room in their wolf den in Montana. Headed straight out to the rendezvous she'd agreed on with Simon to celebrate. She'd settled in by their special creekside spot and waited.

It was one of those beautiful summer days when you could practically taste the blackberries just by walking past or lick sweet honey out of the air. She could still see the bees buzzing happily along, hear the creek babble as it swept merrily by. The perfect place to wait for her lover. Her betrothed. Her mate. She waited...

...and waited, and waited.

He never came, so she'd sought him out in a panic, only to get an icy, awkward stare.

"Listen, Jess, I've been thinking..."

Her jaw had just about hit the ground when Simon confessed it all. That it was only a fling. That he was ready to move on. That he didn't think she'd take all their mating talk seriously, after all.

One of his clanmates had happened by and called him away, and she'd heard every word they exchanged.

"Who was that?" the other bear asked.

"Nobody," Simon had replied. Not *nobody*, as in, that's my sacred secret, but *nobody*, as in, truly a nobody. "Just some she-wolf who won't leave me alone."

The other bear had laughed, and Simon had, too. Even if his laugh sounded forced, she'd just about cried herself into the creek before she finally staggered home. She hadn't uttered a word to her parents because the betrothal was arranged for three years down the line, and by then, she'd figure out some way to wheedle her way out of it. Somehow. Or maybe by then Simon would find a way to get out of it, because obviously, he didn't want her. Jesus, how could she ever face him again?

But she had to face him again, on many more occasions, because her small wolf pack and his tiny bear clan were actually taking the notion of an alliance seriously

21

and mixing more and more. And at each unavoidable gathering, he'd brush her off.

"Nah, she's too skinny for me," he'd said to a friend once. "What would I want with a wolf, anyway?"

Each time, pride made her want to believe his voice had wavered when he spoke, or that his shoulders slumped as if he didn't mean the words. Once he'd even glanced back at her with such pain and sorrow in his eyes, she wanted to cry for him. But a second later, some shadow would come over him. He'd go all cold and stiff and turn away as if she simply didn't exist. As if he'd never really loved her and never really would.

Simon rejected her over and over and over again, until she couldn't help but want to hate him. But she couldn't. Not the Simon she'd known, anyway. The one who used to stroke her cheek with one finger as they lay skin-to-skin on full moon nights when they'd snuck off to be alone. The one who seemed as content to hold her hand and sit by the creek in the sunshine as he was thrilled to get naked with her. The one who looked at her in awe and wonder, as if he'd never really lived, never breathed, never laughed or loved before he met her.

That was her Simon. But this new man... he was a stranger. What had happened? Where had her Simon gone?

She'd endured two years of loving-loathing him until the day he and Soren left. The bear clan had sent the two brothers to learn from their brethren on the East Coast before they were to assume real responsibility at home.

Good riddance, she'd tried convincing herself.

Her wolf, though, counted the days until his return.

But then the rogues had struck, and she never saw Simon again. Until now.

"You've got to believe," Janna repeated, bringing Jessica out of the past.

She blinked at the dilapidated carpet, the skewed pictures on the walls. She believed, all right – that fate was a cruel mistress to make her face Simon Voss again.

Tina strode out of the back room and locked her eyes on Jessica's. "Are you sure you want to do this?"

There it was — her way out. She didn't want this.

I need this. The glaring truth whispered through her mind. *Janna needs it, too.* They needed the jobs. The apartment. They couldn't run any more.

She gave a terse nod. "I want this." A glance in the mirror over the bar told her the lie didn't show, even if her exhaustion did.

Tina studied her for a long, close minute, before nodding back. "All right, then. Follow me."

The raven-haired she-wolf led them down the very same hallway Simon had disappeared into, and Jessica nearly balked. But he'd cleared out by the time she got there. Only Soren and Ty were there, giving her and Janna polite nods when Tina led them to the stairs marked *Private* at the far corner of the room. The stairs creaked to high heaven, as did the bare wooden floors upstairs. Their footsteps echoed down the hallway.

"This is great!" Janna exclaimed.

"Well, it has character," Tina admitted, and that much was true. The floorboards were wide strips of oak, the moldings carved in swirling patterns, and little boxes of colored panes marched across the tops of the window frames. Vibrant green, sunny yellow, silky red. The rooms were big and airy, the ceilings twelve feet high. "But it needs a lot of work."

"We've seen worse," Janna promptly chirped.

And they sure had, though it would be a close contest. Bare light bulbs hung from the ceiling, wallpaper peeled off the walls, and the first two rooms seemed eerily empty.

"The guys are staying in these rooms." Tina pointed. "That one's Soren's."

Jess blinked. The room was bare but for a double mattress on the floor and a bookshelf made from two cinder blocks and a piece of scrap wood. Apart from the paperbacks crowded on the shelves and the clothes piled on a chair in one corner, that was it.

"This one's Simon's." Tina waved, whisking past a closed door. Mercifully closed, as far as Jess was concerned, because she wasn't ready for even another hint of him right now.

His scent crawled all over her and clung to her clothes as she hurried past. *Don't you remember how you loved him?* the scent seemed to say. *How he loved you?*

"That's the only working bathroom, I'm sorry to say." Tina motioned toward a door on the left.

The smell of lemon cleaner was strong there, and Jessica took a good whiff, trying to eradicate Simon's scent.

"Oh, an antique claw-foot tub. Nice," Janna said.

Jess shook her head. Only her sister could overlook the rust stains to appreciate that.

The floorboards creaked as they turned two corners into the rear section of the apartment.

"These are the best rooms for you, I think," Tina said, leading the way. "Sort of in their own little wing. Nice and quiet and at the back, away from the street."

Away from the bears, Jess wanted to add. As far away as possible.

"I love the windows." Janna nodded at the arched windows opening on to a totally different view. There was a parking lot back there in the inner square of the block, but a clutch of trees, too. An alley ran down the back, and beyond...

"Wow. Great view."

That, even Jessica's jaded mind had to agree with. The hills seemed closer somehow, and they were blanketed by a patchwork of pine forest she wouldn't have believed could exist in Arizona.

There were three rooms in that rear section, and as Tina said, set apart in their own wing. So other than sharing the bathroom with the men, they'd have their privacy.

"This can be mine, that can be yours, and the one in the middle can be our living room." Janna's whole face lit up, imagining it.

Jess did her best to imagine, too. Maybe if they got some furniture from the thrift shop, they could get by. Well, maybe if they earned enough first. For now, the lumpy mattresses and crooked closet shelves would have to do.

"I have some sheets in the car," Tina said. "And I'm sure we can rustle up some furniture."

"It'll be great," Janna assured her, sitting down on the mattress and bouncing around like a six-year-old. "It is great. Isn't it, Jess?"

Jessica nodded on cue, glad there wasn't a mirror to check this time. "Great." She thought of Simon, somewhere on the ground floor beneath her, and forced a smile instead of a frown. "It'll be great."

Chapter Four

It wasn't great, but Jessica managed to get through the first day...somehow.

The start was surprisingly easy because Tina dragged them away for a quick shopping trip once she saw how little they had in the way of clothes and threw in a load of groceries, to boot. All on her tab.

"We'll pay you back," Jessica swore. "I swear we will."

Tina's calm eyes did wonders to put her at ease. "I'm sure you will. Don't worry."

"Um, shouldn't we get back to help with lunch?" she tried.

Tina shook her head. "The boys have managed so far..."

Boys? Even in human form, the bear brothers were the size of linebackers.

"They'll manage one more day. Don't worry."

Those last two words, Tina repeated again and again, but Jessica still worried. A lot, and not about the brothers managing lunch.

By the time Tina got them back to the saloon and waved good-bye, it was four o'clock. The good news was, Simon had disappeared on some urgent business, which left only his older brother to deal with. She barely knew

Soren, who'd always been busy learning the ins and outs of clan leadership from his grandfather, but the basics of what she remembered were the same. He was a man of few words who let body language do the talking — mostly in the form of wide-footed stances that screamed, *Alpha bear! Pass at your own risk!* For all his gruff, monosyllabic instructions, though, he was also surprisingly polite. For a grizzly bear, at least.

"Fridge, sink, stove. Watch you don't burn yourself," he grunted during a tour of the massive kitchen between the front and back rooms of the saloon. "Harry." He pointed to the cook, an older, near-deaf wolf shifter, like the man was another pot or pan.

Harry flashed them a toothless smile and went right back to prepping burgers for the day.

"Keys," Soren pointed to a nail on the wall and led them out back.

Jess was starting to see why Tina figured a couple of friendly waitresses might help business at the saloon.

"Smoker. Mine. Don't touch." Soren waved at the contraption in a fenced-off area just outside the back door. "Please," he added as an afterthought, then strode on.

Jess lingered over the metal barrel for a second, relishing the smell of smoked ribs. If they tasted anywhere near as good as they smelled, the saloon might have a chance at turning a profit, after all. She made a mental note to advertise ribs on the sidewalk chalkboard out front. In big, bold letters.

Soren plowed on with Jess and Janna on his heels. "Beer fridge. Don't get locked in."

There were more *don't's* than *do's* on his list, but okay, she could live with that.

"Is there an alarm?" Janna asked.

Soren stared at her. His furrowed brow said, *I'm the alarm.*

The funny thing was, he put Jess at ease. Maybe there was an upside to working for a couple of grouchy bears. She'd been looking over her shoulder ever since fleeing Montana, but here... Maybe she wouldn't have to fear for her life here. Only for her heart.

"Simon tends the bar," Soren went on, lumbering back inside.

Her nerves twisted right back into a knot. That was the part she was dreading. As a waitress, she'd have constant interaction with Simon. But one thing at a time, right?

"Questions?" Soren asked.

"What do you do?" Janna — gutsy Janna — asked.

"Smoked ribs." He glared, but it seemed to be aimed at fate rather than her sister. "Paperwork. Orders. Closing up."

The sisters exchanged glances. Okay, one less bear to deal with in the minute-to-minute operation of the place. They'd both waitressed before. They could handle that.

"You all set?" Soren asked.

Apparently, that was the extent of his tour.

"Um, aprons?" Jessica ventured.

"Notepads?" Janna added. "Specials of the day? Cleaning supplies?"

Soren's eyes narrowed. His grim face folded into a deeper frown.

Jessica grabbed her sister's elbow and steered her toward the front as the bear shifter's eyes grew darker still. "We'll figure it out. Right, Janna?" She jabbed her sister in the ribs.

"Ow!" Janna protested. "I mean, right."

Soren nodded once and disappeared out back.

Old Harry the cook seemed like the safer person to aim their questions at, so they did and tried their best to get oriented to the job.

Once the first few customers trickled in, there was so much to do, so much to figure out, that she didn't notice when Simon first appeared behind the bar. But the second she noticed, well...

He might have been a part of that massive structure himself, the way he stood and stared. As if he were carved from wood, like the bear in the mountain scene at the very top. The blue eyes were the only part of him that moved, following her as she worked, then darting away. He stood smack in front of the mirror, and it was almost too much, seeing that much of him at once — the expressionless front, the ridiculously broad back. The thick, sand-colored hair she'd once weaved her fingers through when they kissed.

"Jess!" Janna hissed, snapping her out of her daze. "Customer. Go."

Clear, concise directions were about all her mind could process just then.

She pasted a smile on, got the customer's order, and froze when she turned to the bar.

Bar. Simon. Drinks...

Thank God for her sister, who grabbed the drink orders out of her hand and took them to Simon like he was just another bartender in just another bar.

Jess cringed at the thought. Maybe that's all she was to Simon — just another former lover. A guy like him had to have had more than his fair share.

30

The next time she glanced back, though, his gaze was on her again, and it seemed to stay there all night. Even when she studiously ignored him, she could feel his gaze on her back. And damn it, her wolf panted with pleasure.

Mine! Mate!

The wolf didn't get it. And she didn't get *him*. Did he despise her so much that he had to obsess about her now?

"You do the food, I'll do the drinks," Janna said in her next sweep past.

And just like that, they got a system going. One that kept the customers happy and Jessica as far away from the bar as she could manage without leaving the saloon — or preferably, the state. But the work kept her busy, especially after Janna darted out to the sidewalk and announced, "Spare ribs!" to a tangle of cowboys striding down the street. Before long, beer flowed, ribs were chomped down to the bone, and raucous laughter rang out through the open doors to the street. With the onset of night, the temperature dropped, and a pleasant breeze worked its way inside, along with more customers, drawn by the noise of the first group.

"Nothing like business to bring more business," Janna murmured with a satisfied smile.

It wasn't exactly a stampede, but it kept them busy. Busy enough to run out of ribs, though no one seemed to care much as long as the booze flowed. The customers were all men, but they stayed just this side of rowdy, and all of them were polite enough.

"Another beer, honey?"

"How about dessert?"

There was no dessert, but she sold them an extra order of fries and made another mental note on what was

31

becoming a long list.

The only other shifter who drifted through the saloon was a state cop, Kyle Williams — a member of Twin Moon pack and another badass shifter who could silence a room with one broody look. He came in, tipped his hat at her and Janna, and gave every guy in the place a slow, pointed look-over. When he left after a few quiet words with Simon, the whole place seemed to exhale.

Not long after, Soren made his second appearance of the night. The first had come a few hours earlier, when things were in full swing. He'd had a good look around, then disappeared silently out back. This time, though, he planted himself right next to the bar, folded his tree-trunk arms over his chest, and announced the last call.

Last call, his stance told every customer, *or else.*

She'd never seen a quieter group of drinkers file out of a bar, or any more polite.

"Thank you, honey."

"Goodnight, sweetheart."

The customers even tipped their hats. Left healthy tips, too. Some of the best she'd ever earned.

She glanced back at the bar, where both brothers stood in tight-lipped command, and it occurred to her that maybe Simon hadn't just been glaring at her all night.

"Goodnight, darling," one of the cowboy-types called and immediately shrank back at the growl coming from the bar.

She whipped around to study Simon, whose murderous eyes ordered the man out the door, and fast.

A warm, secure feeling settled over her weary body as her wolf side went all sappy again. Hadn't it gotten the memo about being tough?

Our mate takes care of us. Protects us.

He lied to us, Jess wanted to retort, but she couldn't quite bring herself to. Not when his gaze turned to her and glowed just a little bit. The way it used to, all those years ago, before things went wrong.

Did he still care? Did he still feel?

A cloud came over his face, and he went straight back to that impassive prison-guard look he'd had all night.

"Come back soon." Janna ushered the last customers out the door.

Jessica leaned against a table, suddenly wiped out.

"You. You." Soren pointed at her, then Janna. "Good job. Go to bed."

"Not before we count the tips," Janna shot back. Jessica had always been the no-nonsense, ballsy one, but for once, their roles were reversed. "Ten percent for the bar, five for the house, right?"

Simon shook his head and even Soren looked surprised when he said, "Tips are all yours tonight."

Janna let out a whoop and jiggled her full pockets. "Awesome!"

Soren nodded his agreement. "Now get going."

"But the cleanup..." Jess protested, despite the throbbing in her feet.

"We'll get it tonight." He nodded at Simon. "You can do tomorrow."

She looked around the unwiped tables, the dirty dishes that needed clearing. Didn't want to even think about the toilets, which wouldn't get any cleaner on their own. "But..."

"Tomorrow," Soren ordered. "Go to bed."

She should have protested a little more, but her knees were buckling by then and a glance in the mirror showed a ghost of her usual self. Or rather, a ghost of the ghost she'd become these last few months. God, when had she become so thin, so worn?

"Thanks," she managed and wobbled toward the back.

"Goodnight!" Janna called, walking along Jessica's left side, blocking her from Simon.

And God, she'd never appreciated her sister as much as she did tonight.

"Goodnight," Soren answered.

"Goodnight," Jess murmured as they went past the bar.

She couldn't see Simon, and she swore she didn't hear him speak, but she could feel the bass of his voice rumble in her bones when he growled his reply.

"Goodnight."

Chapter Five

"What do you think?" Soren asked once they heard the women's weary footsteps creak overhead.

Simon looked around the saloon, then poured himself half a glass of whiskey and downed it in one gulp. He spent a long time sucking on the aftertaste, reeling from the hit. Or maybe just reeling from his night.

What did he think?

It was heaven. It was hell. Having Jessica close — impossibly close. Watching her quick stride, her easy smile. Even if it was aimed at other people, it still put him in knots. The way her hair flowed over her shoulders, the way her brow would scrunch briefly when she added up a tab, then loosened when she saw her tip. He'd watch and let himself pretend that nothing had ever happened. That she was his again.

His bear vacillated all night between the calming, happy glow that always fell over him when she was near and craving her so badly he wanted to pull her out back and kiss her senseless — for starters. Exactly the way they'd done once, ages ago. They'd gone out together and danced a few numbers — well, she danced, he concentrated on not stomping on her feet. And when he couldn't take it any more, he'd dragged his giggling mate out the back door and consumed her in kisses that he couldn't, wouldn't stop. They'd ended up doing it on an empty beer pallet right in a parking lot, with Jess seated on the edge with her legs wrapped around him while he drove into her again and again. His bear had howled the whole time, *Mate! Mate!*

Damn bear had gone on and on that way, even when they were long spent and driving home. Filled his mind with all kinds of crazy thoughts, like a cabin at the edge of the woods filled with her laughter, his joy, and a couple of cubs.

Damn bear had made him convince his grandfather that a wolf might even make a suitable mate for a bear. And it all looked so good, until everything came crashing down.

"You're right," his grandfather said. "Our clan and the wolf pack are both small. An alliance might be just what we need."

Imagine his surprise when his grandfather had announced his decision with the whole council of elders looking on. "I have spoken with the wolf pack, and they agree. The older Macks daughter—"

That was Jessica, and his soul had been singing inside, knowing what he would hear next.

"Shall be betrothed to one of our own clan. Voss blood, mixing with new blood."

Voss. That was him. His bear tapped a happy dance. He and Jess had done it! They'd overcome the odds. Managed to get permission from two stubborn, old-fashioned shifter clans. They had a future together!

"They shall join in three years..." his grandfather had gone on.

The wait didn't thrill him, but he could live with it. It did make sense for him to get a handle on the family lumber business first. That way, he could support Soren when it was his time to take over the clan. Soren could manage overall clan business while Simon ran the mill. That had been laid out since they were kids, and that was fine with him. As long as he could keep seeing Jessica, the wait didn't matter.

"...when our two clans shall come together and celebrate the mating of Jessica Macks and Soren Voss."

Simon's soaring emotions had crash-landed right there. "Wait, what was that?"

He blurted that out in front of everyone, even though the younger generation wasn't supposed to utter a word at council meetings.

"What was that?" Soren had barked, too, and even though *he* was allowed to speak as heir apparent, their grandfather still glared.

"The eldest Macks girl mated to the eldest Voss," the old man growled. "Soren."

And just like that, Simon's whole world caved in.

It didn't matter how much he begged or pleaded or raged. Didn't matter that an alliance was his idea. Didn't matter what he wanted.

"It has been decided," his grandfather had said, and that was that.

"Did anyone ask her?" he yelled, then went slack-jawed at his grandfather's shrug.

"We asked her father."

Christ. Apparently, wolves were as medieval as bears when it came to marrying off their young. What a fool he'd been to think it would be any other way.

"Did anyone bother telling her?"

Blank looks said nobody had, and he'd been too much of a coward to do it himself.

Soren had sworn up and down that he wouldn't go through with it. He'd even confided that he already had a mate of his own. A woman he'd known since he was a kid and courted ever since. It was only a question of time before he asked the elders for permission to take her as his bride.

"We'll figure something out. We will," Soren swore.

Wishful thinking, and both of them knew it. Soren had no chance in hell of ever getting permission to take his destined mate — a human, no less.

"And that will be that," their grandfather, the clan leader, had announced.

Simon had just about melted into the floor. There was no way out. He'd have to live his whole life with his true love mated to another. To his own brother!

They'd both found their own solutions, he and Soren. Soren bottled up, tight as a bear in winter, and barely uttered a word after that. He threw himself at clan duty with a vengeance, except when the irresistible pull of his mate had him steal away to spend time with her.

And Simon... What the hell could he do? If Jessica loved him the way he loved her, she'd die before she mated with his brother. That, or she'd run, and the wolves would hunt her down and drag her back. Her own pack, or worse, one of those marauding packs of wolves bent on preserving the racial purity of shifters. The kind who exercised their own brand of vigilante justice by burning alive anyone found to have crossed species lines.

No. For her own sake, he had to keep Jess within the protection of both their clans. She'd be safe as long as she stayed near Black River. Safe, as long as she was with Soren.

The thought made him sick, but it was the truth. He'd have to find a way to make Jess accept that they could never be together.

Which was when it dawned on him. He couldn't allow her to love him. In fact, they'd both be better off if she hated him, right?

God, he'd been young and stupid, thinking that. It was torture, pushing her away. Bile rose in his throat every time he forced himself to blurt out some awful lie or insult, but he'd told himself he was doing it for her. If she hated him, she might find happiness with Soren. So what if he bound himself in a living hell? If Jess hated him, maybe he could handle losing her.

"Christ, those she-wolves know how to hustle," Soren murmured at his side.

He dragged his thoughts back to the present and to the saloon. Yes, Jess and Janna had been great. They'd been more than great. The saloon had hummed along smoothly. Business had been good.

And Jess had hated him the whole time.

Fuck, fuck, fuck. He'd worked so hard at making her despise him; it had worked. And now that the laws that had denied them their happiness were no longer a factor — the clan was gone, just like her pack, fallen victim to the very rogues he'd underestimated — he was still fucked. Yes, he mourned his family. Yes, he mourned hers. And yes, he'd hunted down the wolves who had annihilated both their clans just before he and Soren returned. But it was all for nothing.

His mate hated him. Drew back from him. She couldn't even meet his eyes, for Christ's sake. He could have her, but he couldn't have her.

The irony could have killed him. It very nearly did. He'd engineered his own living hell. His own damnation.

Soren smacked him on the back and pointed to the saloon.

"Get going. Clean up."

Simon took the first of many stiff, aching steps, telling himself he'd go find a cave to curl up and die in later. For now, he'd do what he had to do.

Which was what, exactly? He examined his options as he wiped down the bar, ran the glasses through the dishwasher, and cleaned out the sink. His mate would never accept him. His life was over.

But hers wasn't.

He stole a glance out the front window, trying to catch a glimpse of the stars. Ursa Major or Minor or really, any constellation that could show him the path to a miracle solution. But the stars shunned him as they'd done for the past couple of months. Practically sneered at him. *Figure it out yourself.*

And eventually, he did. He realized what he had to do. He had to give Jess this chance to get back on her feet after all she'd endured. Help her save money, then move on to something better than this. Maybe even someone better than him.

His bear rumbled inside, but he just shook his head. If he really loved Jess, that's what he'd do.

He'd do what he had to do, for her.

Chapter Six

Jessica dragged herself out of bed — or rather, off the surprisingly comfy queen-size mattress on the floor of her un-
furnished room, where she'd slept ridiculously well. Better than she had in years, it seemed. She listened for any
sound of bear before dashing in and out of the bathroom
as quickly as she could. But even there, she got waylaid
by the scent of Simon's aftershave and towel — the towel
she absolutely, positively, did not inhale deeply from once
or twice. Another second's delay came from the mental
image of his perfect, naked body crowding that claw-foot
tub...

She snapped herself out of that with a shake of the
head and gave herself the same stern lecture in the mirror
she'd been trying for years — *He does not love you; there-
fore, you do not love him* — and finally scurried downstairs. Bears were notoriously late risers, and her sister
Janna, too, so she had all of the downstairs to herself for
a couple of hours.

She'd slept soundly, but then reality hit her all over
again: the crazy situation she found herself in. Seeing
Simon again. Aching for him. Resenting him, then resenting herself. Mourning her family, detesting the rogues
who'd wiped out her small pack.

There was only one way to cope: her own form of

therapy. Cooking and cleaning.

Well, baking, to start with. Something she'd always loved doing with her grandmother as a kid. They'd go berry picking in the woods, then head home and whip up a batch of muffins. She started raiding the saloon kitchen, looking for what she needed. There was a smaller fridge marked *Private*, full of huge quantities of eggs and bacon — which she suspected Simon and Soren shoveled down for breakfast in insane, lumberjack portions — and little else. The cabinets held a supply of flour, though. There was some baking soda doing a poor job of keeping the industrial-sized fridge fresh, plus a little milk and butter. She had the blackberries Tina had bought for her yesterday and the chocolate chips her sister had thrown in with the shopping, too. Sugar in a tin on a shelf on the wall, and even a pinch of vanilla.

In short, she had everything she needed. She scrubbed a rusty muffin tin, spooned in the batter for half a dozen berry and half a dozen berry-chocolate chip muffins, and that was that.

A tear slid down her cheek as she thought about her grandmother and all the loved ones who had been erased from her life. But the memories... no one could take those, right? She wiped her eyes, blinked a few times, and looked around. Work. She needed work to keep her mind off the past.

Harry seemed to keep the kitchen reasonably clean, so she started in the front room of the saloon. She didn't touch the bar, because something told her that was bear territory and she'd better keep clear. Instead, she tackled the spider webs in the corners of the room and between the blades of the overhead fans, then washed the front windows. She snuck in a bite of muffin in between and held on to the taste like it was another part of her past, then rallied herself out front to clean some more. She scrubbed and scrubbed until the morning sun shone in, and she wished she could do the same with her memories. Clear out the bad ones, make room for the sun to shine in. The water in her bucket quickly turned gray, and she headed back to the kitchen for a refill. Leaning over the sink as fresh water ran from the tap, she closed her eyes, and thought about the creek in Montana where she and Simon used to meet. The shade, the summer shadows. The babbling stream. She dug far enough back in her memories that she could almost imagine his soft step behind her.

Her eyes flew open, because there really was a step vibrating through the floor, and she whipped around.

"Simon," she breathed. Or maybe she just thought it because, for a second, her mind went blank. Did she hate him? Love him? Which was it again?

He stood there, filling most of the doorway, wearing nothing but a pair of loose lounge pants. Looking like a bear straight from his winter den, with his hair spiked up on one side and down on the other. He scratched his bare chest with one hand, wiped his eyes with the other. He slid his shoulder up and down the door frame, marking the place as his. The only part of him that seemed truly awake was his sense of smell. His nostrils were wide, sniffing deeply.

"Berries?" he mumbled. The sound vibrated through the floor and slowly, sensually, climbed her legs.

Her heart swelled. Her heart thumped. Her wolf wagged its tail. She'd made her mate happy! He loved her! She'd pleased him with—

Her human side slammed on the brakes. God, her

43

wolf was as bad as her parents with their old-fashioned ways. Her life was not about pleasing men, least of all this one. She was an independent, self-sufficient, modern woman who could damn well...

He scratched his jaw, and memories of nuzzling that very stubble flooded her. Memories of the cave, all those years ago. It had been so cold in the blizzard that she'd had no choice but to stumble in. And then Simon had come along and their little shelter heated right up. First with anger, as they faced each other down, then with a whole different kind of heat once they'd finally agreed to huddle for warmth. He'd curled his bulk silently around her back and laid absolutely, positively still for a while. The only movement was the faint puff of air against her cheek. For a few minutes, at least, because she couldn't help but sigh and wiggle back against him.

And then he'd come snuffling carefully closer. Sniffing, then nuzzling, as if he couldn't resist her any more than she could resist him. He'd scraped his chin slowly, deliciously over the soft skin of her cheek in long, possessive strokes, and it lit every nerve ending in her body on fire. Sent her brain right out the door and let instinct take over. It wasn't long before she pulled his arm over her side and around her front, because it was more comfortable that way. And it wasn't long after his fingers first touched down on her breast that she turned in his arms and found his lips for their first, soft kiss. A kiss that led to another, and another, and—

Jess snapped upright, jolting out of memories and back into the kitchen. Christ, what had set that off?

"Berry muffins," she said, planting her feet wide. She'd hold her ground. Stare him down. Let him know she was as over him as he was over her.

Or fake it, at least.

"I made them," she added for good measure. Daring him.

His ears twitched. His lips parted just a little bit. His eyes focused directly on her. They roamed down, then up, then down again. She had the distinct impression Simon was going through exactly what she had been, a minute before. *Do I love her? Hate her?*

Love! her wolf cheered. *Love!*

Bit by bit, Simon masked himself in that impassive expression that was his armor, his shield, his castle, and retreated within the walls. "Can I have one?"

He didn't bark out. Didn't demand. He just asked, almost like a normal person would. But if she looked — really looked — she saw the bear inside, wide-eyed and hungry, desperate to get out.

She folded her arms over her chest, showing him she could play tough guy, too. Let him wonder and worry and think the way she had through all of the previous night. Even if it was only for a few seconds, damn it, she'd get a teensy, tiny bit of revenge.

"Sure, boss." She kicked out that second word just to keep him on his toes. *Yes, you can have one, but only because I have no choice.*

The moment she thought it, her body hardened, because it was true. She had no choice. Hadn't had a choice for a long, long time. She stuck her jaw out a little so it wouldn't wobble, then turned back to the sink. She turned off the water and stared into her bucket like it was a wishing well. If only she had a penny...

He came closer with slow, heavy steps. Closer. Even closer, and she shut her eyes closed, imagining the perfect happy end. His arms would wrap around her, and he'd pull her against his chest then whisper *I'm sorry* and *I love you* and *Please, please, give me a second chance.* He'd kiss her ear like he used to, and she would turn and kiss him back. Go from kissing to touching and to wrapping her legs around—

Simon came up right behind her, and hope jumped into her throat.

He made a little sound. A barely perceptible, bottom-of-the-earth growl. The scent of desire steamrolled the muffin smell aside and spread through the warm kitchen like a pleasant haze. Her wolf nearly howled.

Then a sharp inhale, an angry puff, and he sidestepped toward the muffins.

And, *Poof!* Her fantasy vanished. Just like that.

Jess picked up the bucket so fast, water sloshed out the top. She grabbed her washcloth and hurried for the door.

"Jess." His voice stopped her cold. A voice from the past, because it was soft and wistful and sweet.

She turned around slowly and there was Simon, looking like a man who needed a good, long sleep and not a man who'd just come out of one. Weary. Defeated. Struggling to find the strength to go on.

"Thanks," he whispered.

A word. Practically a speech in bear-talk. But it was enough.

She nodded and walked away slowly rather than fleeing as fast as she could. Victory. A very small victory for her pride, if nothing else.

She went back to scrubbing windows and managed to will her mind blank. Of everything that is, except for muffin recipes she'd be trying out for her bear over the next couple of days.

She corrected herself quickly. Er, not for her bear. For her boss. Just her boss. And her sister and the saloon and everyone else.

Her wolf licked its lips. *Yeah, right.*

Chapter Seven

Two weeks went by like that, and Simon went right on vacillating between heaven and hell.

Heaven was the sight of Jessica, bright and shiny and energetic, with the morning sun glowing on her hair. Heaven was the honey-lavender scent of her, a minute after she cleared the shower and padded down the hall, thinking he was asleep when he was listening to her. Heaven was in the muffins his bear kept insisting she'd baked just for him, even though she shared them with everyone else.

But hell was never far behind. Hell was the sight of her gray-blue eyes firmly fixed on the floor. The way her smile vanished when she turned away from a customer and glanced toward the bar. Hell was having to head upstairs after a long day's work and not being able to follow instinct around the bends of the hallway, all the way over to her room.

Hell and damnation. He lived them each and every day.

Occasionally, they'd both be so busy that they'd forget, and their bodies would drift together, only to skitter apart. As if their animal sides knew just what they wanted, while the humans kept stubbornly apart. He'd be filling drinks behind the bar at peak time; she'd pop in to wash her hands at the sink. And somehow, the space between would slip away so their arms could graze, and a brush fire would race through his blood. A primal rhythm would start to beat in his bones. A smile would build on his lips—

And Jess would jolt and hurry away and not look back.

So nothing was different, though nothing was quite the same. Of course, it wouldn't be, with two she-wolves slowly taking over the saloon. Jess and her sister were like a pair of tornadoes determined not to leave anything in its place. Some things for better, some things for worse.

It started with cleaning, which was mostly good. Other than them throwing out the stuffed beaver that used to hang in the corner by the bar, claiming it was disgusting and moldy and a travesty to shifters everywhere.

Well, okay, he'd give them that, even if he did hate beavers. Snobby, intellectual little things.

The next thing they did was number the tables. What that was all about, he didn't know. There were only ten tables in the whole place. A couple on the right, a few in the middle, and the booths at the side. Who needed numbers?

Wolves, apparently. Jess and Janna numbered the tables and even rearranged a few, chattering something about traffic patterns and light and views.

He looked around. What views?

"Three Cokes for table five," Jess would say, handing off the drink order to her sister. Avoiding him, of course.

"Three Cokes for table five," Janna would echo as she slapped down her tray.

He'd squint out over the saloon and wonder which was table five, because it wasn't like they'd actually labeled the tables or given him a chart or anything. They had it memorized. A damn good thing he didn't have to deliver the drinks he poured.

And that was just the tip of the iceberg. No, a goddamn avalanche, and it was all he and Soren could do to keep up.

The menu grew the way hair products multiplied in the bathroom they all shared, which was fine, in principle. In practice, his bear wasn't so sure. Like the third morning of the avalanche, when he'd woken from a beautiful dream in which he and Jess were rolling in a mountain meadow, naked, feeding each other berries — a weird combination, but yeah, a damn good dream — and stumbled downstairs to find the kitchen packed with racks and racks of muffins. The air practically crystallized with their sweet smell, but there was no sign of Jess. He snagged a muffin that just pleaded for him to show some mercy and gobble it up, and when he bit in, he groaned. Sweet, juicy blueberries exploded in his mouth and transported him home to Montana. He stood there savoring it until he stomped himself into action and headed out front. Still no sign of Jess, so he continued out the open front door, where he stalled out at the sight of her squatting beside a sidewalk chalkboard, spelling out the saloon's latest deal.

Coffee and muffin to go! Her script was clear and inviting. *$6 combo.*

"Coffee and what?" he yelped, suddenly awake.

She jolted, as she always did, and stopped humming. Stood slowly. Defiantly. All wolf, all pride. Probably composing her face as she turned, putting on that icy expression she always socked him with.

Yep, there it was. And God, she was something, even as Miss Frost.

"Muffins." She drew the word out like a dare.

Muffins? She was selling *his* muffins?

"This is a saloon, not a bakery."

"A saloon that can use every customer it can get," she retorted, stepping back to check her work. She knelt again, wiped out the $6, and changed it to $5.99.

"Who cares about a penny?"

"Believe me, it works."

A slip of paper fluttered out of her hand, and he caught it flying down the sidewalk like a tumbleweed.

"What's this?"

"Flyers. I put them in the bag with the muffins. What we really need is printed napkins, though."

We? His bear chuffed with hope.

He glanced at the slip of paper, trying not to get distracted. *Ribs, burgers, & beers on tap at the Blue Moon Saloon. Thursday special.*

"We have a Thursday special?"

"We do now." Jessica nodded and waved to someone down the street. A guy with a whole plate of muffins in hands. "See you, Mike!"

Mike? "Who the hell is Mike?"

"Thank you, sweetheart. See you later," the asshole called back. The short, bald asshole disappearing into a store two buildings down.

"Mike," Jess said firmly. "Of Mike's hardware."

He stared at her. "Don't tell me you're giving muffins away." *Giving my muffins away*, he nearly said.

"Think about it. We're right between Mike's Hardware and the nearest parking lot. When the spots on the street fill up, most of his customers walk right by here."

"Yeah, when we're closed."

"If we open half an hour earlier—"

She wanted him to get up half an hour earlier?

"—we'll get his mid-morning rush. And if Mike and his guys are all licking their fingers and saying how good the Blue Moon Muffins are..." She smiled in satisfaction. "...his clients will become our clients."

She left out the *dummy* at the end of that sentence, but he saw it on the tip of her tongue. Apparently, her wolf had found her sassy side again. He watched in silence as she squatted over the chalkboard again. Now what?

Soren padded out beside him, yawning. Watched her write. Scratched his chest.

They both stood there a long time after Jess rose, gave a satisfied nod, and marched back inside.

"Gluten-free?" Soren examined the muffin he was holding. He took a bite, washed it down with a sip of coffee in a paper cup, and munched thoughtfully. "Raspberry chocolate. Not bad. Not bad."

Jesus. Whose side was Soren on, anyway?

He spent a good five minutes scraping up and down the doorframe after that, trying to reclaim the upper hand.

And that was just the start. It got worse, or better, depending how you viewed change. The chalkboard by the door was filled with colorful, girly handwriting, starting with *Smoked Spare Ribs* in letters decorated with little flames. Then came burgers. Lots and lots of burgers. There seemed to be no limit to their imagination when it

came to burgers. And two she-wolves were more dangerous than one.

"What we need is a theme," Janna had announced
one night, speaking with authority. "Theme burgers."

What the fuck was a theme burger?

"Diamondback burger!" Janna shouted in inspira-
tion. "Harry can sear a diamond pattern into the bun
on the grill."

"Mesa burger," Jess said, and Janna wrote it down.
They loved writing things down. "Open bun style, with
cheese on top."

Which didn't sound too bad, once he pictured it.

"Hungry cowboy burger," Jess went on. "With bacon."

"Oh! Oh! I got it." Janna bounced as she scribbled
away furiously. "Hungry bear burger!"

Simon was about to protest, but she went on.

"With barbecue sauce!"

Soren tilted his head and licked his lips.

"Hungry works well," Jess decided.

They made him drool, just talking about it. He
watched them brainstorm one new burger after another.
Watched as the ideas practically lifted them off the
ground. Avocado burgers. Bacon cheeseburgers. Feta
spinach burgers.

"Big beef burger!" Janna cried happily.

They were so excited. So alive. So full of energy and
excitement, like a couple of kids at their first lemonade
stand, that a little of it seeped over into him. Maybe he
should look into some more microbreweries, more beers
to offer on tap...

He shuffled a little behind the bar, pretending to
be busy when he was watching the sisters. Maybe it

didn't matter if no one ever bought a veggie burger. Just the idea seemed to lift them up. Two sisters who'd been through so much. From what Tina had confided, they'd witnessed the destruction of their pack. They'd been there the night of the slaughter and barely escaped. They'd suffered a lot more than he had.

But slowly, surely, they were moving on.

Soren was watching too, and his solemn expression said he was thinking the same thing. They exchanged wary glances. Shit, maybe they ought to finally move on, too.

Simon studied the suds in the freshly washed sink and chewed that one over for a while. There was just one catch. Jess and Janna had fought for their lives and escaped. He and Soren hadn't escaped anything. Especially not the guilt that came with knowing they'd failed to be there for their clan when they were needed most. Soren had lost his destined mate in the attack. He'd failed her, just like Simon had failed Jess.

Except Jess had survived. And there she was, hating him, and moving on with her life.

Soren strode away, heading back to the kitchen to prep another batch of ribs, and Simon had to wonder. Did women move on better than men did? Or were wolves just better at it than bears?

He sighed a little. The sooner he could get Jess out and on her way to something better, the better off he'd be. Somewhere far, far away, so his bear couldn't scent her, sense her, long for her all the time.

His bear rumbled inside. *Just you try taking my mate away. Just you try.*

He shoved the bear aside. What Jess and Janna needed was something better than a small-town saloon.

Something that was a better fit for them. Better for them in every way, actually, because he was only thinking about their welfare, right? Somehow, he had to get through the next few weeks. Enough for the sisters to realize how unsuited they were for the saloon business and find something better — ideally, somewhere on the other side of the continent — and move on. Alaska. Maybe even Australia. Whatever. Out of sight, out of mind, right?

His bear let out a long, low growl.

The problem was, they weren't unsuited for the saloon business. Not in the least. Janna was outgoing and friendly and funny. Great with the customers and with his cranky brother, too. She even seemed to *enjoy* waiting tables, which made about no sense. Not only that, but she had a way of hauling customers in from out on the street, like she could see what food they liked from the expression on their faces.

"We've got great burgers, you know." She'd grab the tourists with that line and finish them off with, "Local beef. And we've got the perfect microbrew to go with it, too."

One of the few microbrews they carried. They really ought to get more.

"Quick coffee? Grilled sandwich to go?" That's what she'd offer to the contractor-types who hurried from the parking lot to Mike's Hardware. The idea was Jessica's, the execution all Janna. The contractors would order grilled sandwiches on the way into the hardware store, then pick them up on their way out. The old-fashioned register that sat at the left end of the bar dinged merrily with every sale.

"Fifteen beers on tap," Janna would call to the horse-wrangling types, like Cole, who'd come to occupy a semipermanent spot at the bar. Between her looks and her almost-but-not-quite-flirty voice, it worked every time.

Jess was more reserved, but she was a pro at keeping everything moving without seeming rushed. Every water jug was topped off before it got under half full, every table re-set in record time. She had the dishwasher emptied before he noticed the cycle was through and the tables cleaned the second customers were out the door. And zoom — she'd be all over the next customers in a flash.

"What can I get you?" She'd lean over them with her notepad and pen, practically exuding *your food will be great, the service efficient* vibes.

"What can I get you?" Jess would ask, and his head would whip around every time.

You, he wanted to answer. *You can get me you. You and the past before all of this happened and we still smiled and laughed and loved. When we'd meet up by the creek and leave the world behind. When the future was more than another day in hell.*

"What can I get you?" she asked, aiming the question at a couple who'd just wandered in, not him.

He looked at the customers. A nice, clean-cut couple wearing loafers that labeled them as out-of-staters. That was the other thing. Jess and Janna had started to pull in a whole new clientele. Simon scanned the place, taking count. Maybe he and his brother were meaner-looking than they meant to be, because they'd never had so many... well, *normal* types in the Blue Moon before. A pair of businessmen sat in a booth to one side, tapping notes into tablets and comparing charts. A family — with kids! — ventured through the door, and Jess had them doodling on napkins in two seconds flat.

"Crayons," she hissed, slapping down their drink order. She'd finally started bringing him the occasional drink order after about a week on the job. "Put that on the list. We need crayons. Placemats, too."

We? Crayons? The words were foreign to his ears.

His bear, though, loved it. Loved having her only a foot away. Loved the click of her shoes, because even if she hurried into the kitchen, she'd have to hurry back out again. Her lavender scent would mingle slowly with all the spices in the kitchen, then waft out again on her next trip past. The scent of a fresh mountain stream. The scent of home.

Crayons. His bear nodded inside. *Kids. Nice.*

Simon decided it would be safer not to explore whose kids the bear was thinking about — the ones at table three or five or whatever it was, or the ones he wanted to have with Jessica someday. He gritted his teeth. The woman was impossible.

"What list?" he growled, but she had already whisked past.

There couldn't be a list, because a list meant she was investing herself in the saloon, and that just wouldn't work.

Somehow, he had to get her out and on with her life. So he could get on with his.

Not forbidden anymore, his bear chuffed.

Her ramrod back, her icy eyes, though, said the opposite. Practically screamed it, in fact.

Chapter Eight

It was Saturday night, and the rodeo was in town. Which meant the talk was all bulls and riders, the ongoing drought, and the fool hiker who'd nearly burned the forest down with a cigarette butt. And yes, business was slow. Slow enough for Simon to have way too much time to think about Jess.

About him and Jess, too. Worse still, about himself.

But mostly, about her.

Somehow, they'd reached an equilibrium of sorts, and part of him wanted to imagine that they could keep it up that way. He could pretend not to love her while she went on quietly hating him without it interrupting work or the other parts of his life.

One minor detail, his bear pointed out. *We have no life.*

Which was pretty much true. All he had was work. All he really wanted was work.

And Jess, his bear grunted back. *Jess, Jess, Jess.*

Stubborn beast. Greedy beast, because she deserved better than him. Stupid beast, to think she might ever take a failure of a bear back. He had a better chance of winning the Arizona State Lottery than winning her over, especially after what happened next.

Because he goofed. Big-time.

The phone rang. That was it. That's what set it all off. Just the stupid phone ringing and him reacting too fast.

He'd been on edge all night because Ty Hawthorne had stopped by earlier and pulled him and Soren aside for a little chat. If "a little chat" was the right term for the pointed glare and thunderous silences of the Twin Moon alpha.

"We got word from Colorado," Ty started in a voice so low, Simon wanted to stoop to hear. "That band of rogues has been asking around."

Simon went stiff all over while Ty's laser glare drilled into him as if *he* were the goddamn rogue.

No one had to clarify which rogues Ty meant. There were always a few afoot, but only one group that could truly concern the Twin Moon alpha. Blue Bloods — the band that had annihilated the bear clan and wolf pack in Montana.

Ty leaned closer. "I thought you said you killed them."

Ripped them to pieces was more like it, Simon wanted to say. He and Soren had returned to Black River too late to do anything but witness the carnage, but they'd hunted the rogues down after that. They'd tracked, trapped, and killed every last rogue they could find. It had taken months.

"We killed all we could find," Soren replied in a sharp voice.

"And then?" Ty glared.

Soren looked at the ground. Simon, too. What then? They'd simply stopped hunting because they were empty. They'd caught and killed every one of the rogue wolves involved in killing their clan and Jessica's Black River pack.

The problem was, that handful of rogues was part of a bigger organization that fed off boredom and discontent. Wolf packs were run as strict hierarchies, and young males had three choices. They could fight their way to the top, learn to live as subordinates, or get the hell out. Those who chose the latter roamed in disorganized bands, causing trouble here and there, and groups like the Blue Bloods recruited from among them. But the Blue Bloods weren't as disorganized as the rest. And these days, they didn't seem to just be here and there but everywhere. They didn't dare take on big, powerful packs like Ty's, which was full of alpha males dedicated to their pack and their leader. Instead, the Blue Bloods targeted small, splintered groups of shifters.

Soren grimaced. "We got the rogues responsible."

Ty didn't look impressed. "Yeah, well, there are more."

"There will always be more," Simon threw in.

"More rogues asking about a pair of she-wolves on the run from Black River?" Ty asked.

Simon froze. All this time, he'd considered Blue Moon Saloon a safe place. And it was, for the likes of himself and his brother. But for Jess and Janna...

Shit. They were nominally under the protection of Twin Moon pack, but way, way out on the fringe. A band of determined rogues might just try...

"They wouldn't dare," Soren barked, pulling himself to full height.

Ty blinked back at him from two inches higher up, unimpressed. "I'm sending the boys over tonight. Let them keep an eye out for those two."

Simon barely bit back his protest. Jess wasn't Ty's to protect. She was his. Janna, too. His bear had them firmly seated in his own little clan. Who did Ty think he was?

He glared at the alpha wolf, who socked him with his own hard look. A look that said, *I am the alpha of my pack. I protect them to the death. Who do you think you are?*

All the anger and pride drained out of Simon like a plug had been pulled. Ty was right. He'd let rogues kill his entire clan. He hadn't protected squat.

A failure. A miserable failure of a bear.

"Right," Soren mumbled, grudgingly accepting the idea of Ty's wolves keeping an extra eye on the place. Ty might not have noticed the hurt in Soren's voice, but Simon did. Enough hurt to suggest that Soren had been thinking of Jess and Janna as denmates, too.

Ty Hawthorne stomped out of the saloon, and the two brothers looked at each other. Failures, both of them.

"Back to work," Soren sighed.

So if Simon was on edge that evening, it wasn't his goddamn fault. A good thing business was slow; his bear was ready to throw the first asshole who came along through the front window.

But no such luck. At ten p.m., the last sizable group cleared out, leaving only a handful of customers who were long past dessert. Yes, dessert, because Jess had added apple and key lime pie to the menu a few days ago. And every time she brought a piece out or carried a dirty plate away, she shot him a victorious look.

Take that, bear, her glances seemed to say.

A tough one, Jess. Tough enough to have somehow survived the rogue attack. Tough enough to fight back.

He knew; they'd play-wrestled often enough for him to know what a capable fighter she was. But those tangles had always tipped over into sweet, sweaty sex, not life-and-death. And for all that she'd started to look better than the ghost she'd arrived as, he still wouldn't want to see her up against rogues. Hell, he never wanted to see her up against any kind of threat.

So he kept an eagle eye on the door and made sure every guy in the bar knew she was off-limits. That she was his.

Even if, technically, she wasn't his.

Janna, meanwhile, seemed as chipper and clueless as ever. Which was good, he supposed. Why worry her? Let her flirt with Cole, the lonesome cowboy at the far end of the bar. Janna seemed to have a thing for his type: wounded, mysterious, and, as he'd once heard her whisper to Jess, hotter than hot. Cole wasn't far over thirty, Simon would have guessed, though he drank like an old man looking back on a long and bitter life. A former bull rider, that's what someone had said. Did he even suspect that his waitress could morph into a wolf?

Cole lifted a finger in a signal for another. "One for the road."

Janna whammed her hand on the bar in a karate chop. "Make that a Coke."

Cole groaned, and Simon did, too. "You're supposed to give the customers what they want."

"He wants a Coke," she retorted. "Isn't that right?"

Janna seemed to be working on her own get-Cole-dry crusade, with mixed results. But the cowboy was a sucker for that pretty smile and those big blue eyes. Who wouldn't be?

"Just what I want," Cole sighed, though his eyes were bright. Maybe a little attention from the right woman was all the guy needed. He was too young to let himself get all washed up. Young and tough and scarred, outside and in, it seemed. "A Coke."

Whatever. Simon had enough problems of his own to think about Cole, or what Cole might try with Janna. The cowboy might throw a mean punch — as Simon had found out in a brawl that broke out during opening week — but it was a punch for the good guys. So Cole seemed all right. And if he did try something with Janna, he'd have no chance against her shifter speed and skill. Same for all the guys in the saloon. No real threat for Janna there. The rogues were the threat, and rogues were sneaky bastards who wouldn't just come sauntering in.

He poured Coke into a whiskey glass and slid it down the length of the bar to Cole, who raised it in a silent toast.

The phone rang, and Janna came around the bar to answer it.

"Blue Moon Saloon. This is Janna. Hello?"

And there it was — the moment Simon flipped out and destroyed what had been an otherwise quiet night. One second, he felt calm and in control, if on high alert, and the next...

Janna yelped, because he wrenched the phone straight out of her hand. He all but jumped her to get to it. Slammed it down on the receiver and snarled. Really snarled — at Janna! At sweet, friendly Janna. Janna, who didn't have a clue what kind of danger she was in.

"Are you nuts?" he hissed, barely under his breath.

Janna stood there with her jaw half open, and Simon had just enough time to think, *Oops*, when someone punched him from the side.

He whipped around, expecting Soren, but it was Jess.

Jess, with a fury in her eyes he'd never seen before. Jess, the warrior. Jess, all fed up.

"Don't you dare," she hissed. Her eyes were full of hate. Not that wishy-washy, *I'm trying hard to hate you* look she'd worn over the past couple of weeks, but one-hundred-proof hate. Hate she didn't have to work at. Hate from the bottom of her heart.

Which meant he'd succeeded. Succeeded at last. Jess hated him, so she'd be free to move on.

Funny, all he could feel was ashamed.

But bears didn't show shame. They didn't show fear, especially of a future to be spent broken and alone. They showed anger and power and bluster. So he glared back, just to prove what an idiot he was.

"Don't be a fool," he snarled back.

Her canines extended and pure wolf pride flared in her eyes. "Don't you dare," she repeated, socking him with a glare he'd remember for the rest of his days.

"Don't you—" she started.

If Soren hadn't popped in out of nowhere, she might have shifted to wolf form and attacked him, there and then. And Simon would have been fool enough to shift, too.

Good thing for his glaring, two-hundred-pound brother standing between the two of them.

"Cut it out," Soren barked under his breath, jutting his chin toward the saloon. "Customers."

Thank God no one noticed the cute waitress' fangs extend or the way hair sprouted out all over the bartender's beefy arms. Cole had reached down to retrieve a coaster, so he, too, hadn't seen them. Yet.

Soren took Simon by the collar and shoved him toward the back room. "Out. Now."

Janna rushed toward the customers, holding up a couple of menus to block their line of sight. "Can I get you anything else?"

Simon pushed away from his brother, but he did as he was told. He stomped down the hallway and into the unlit back room, heading for the rear door. Ready to rip it open, take off into the hills, and let his inner bear maraud for a while just to get everything out. But before he got there, his bear dug his heels in.

It's not me who wants to beat up the past, the bear protested. *Not me who fucked it all up.*

He thumped his forehead against the wall and panted there for a minute or two. His bear wasn't the failure. He was. He'd just growled at Jess! His own mate.

His bear groaned mournfully. *Not after what you've done to her. Not any more.*

He slumped against the wall and slid down hopelessly until his ass came to rest on the cold, hard floor, suddenly drained. Like there was an off switch wired into that wall and rubbing against it sapped the last bit of energy he possessed. He sat and stared at his toes, just as he'd done when he'd returned home to find only ash and bone.

Fuck. What had he just done?

Damned himself forever, that's what he'd done.

The light filling the hallway dimmed with a large figure. Soren, tugging Jessica along.

"You," Soren barked, glaring at his pathetic form. Nine Supreme Court justices couldn't deliver a more solemn accusation than his brother did with one word.

"And you." He looked at Jess with a softer expression and motioned her across the room with a firm nod. "Sit."

Simon stared at the floor as she strode stiffly past him, leaned against the wall, and crossed her arms defiantly.

Simon. He looked up, hearing Soren call into his mind. Brothers could do that. Clanmates, too. Not to mention mates, though Jess had long since shut him out of her mind. "Talk."

He didn't want to talk, damn it.

"You want peace?" Soren demanded. "Tell her."

How could he ever tell Jess? Where would he start?

"I have to go," Soren sighed, turning for the door. "Tell her."

Jess glanced at him with an alarmed expression that said, *Tell me what?*

Chapter Nine

Jess steeled herself. It was time to finally face down her bear. She'd rip into him and give him exactly what he deserved. She'd finally, finally speak her mind. She had the words rallied, mustered and ready to attack.

She'd let him have it, all right.

She looked at Simon, but same as always, he didn't meet her eyes. He never did. Nothing she did seemed good enough for him. She could hustle her ass in the saloon morning, noon, and night. She could scrub the place — scrub the toilets, for goodness' sake — and he'd never utter a word. Never reward her with so much as a smile.

And he'd had the nerve to strong-arm her sister! Well, she'd had enough of his grouchy, domineering ways. Had enough of his belittling glances and tight, unhappy lips. She'd had enough of all the derisive comments she imagined hanging on the tip of his tongue. She'd absolutely, positively had enough.

"You—" she started spitting out the attack, but he countered in the most unexpected way.

"Jesus, Jess..." His murmur was full of pain and defeat, and it stopped her cold.

A shaft of pale light fell through the dusty window and into the dim room, lighting up a thousand dancing particles of dust. Beyond it, in shadow, Simon sat, quiet and broken. His voice wasn't angry. More like fearful. His eyes slid shut, extinguishing the twin, shiny points.

Her heart lurched. She was ready for angry or mean or harsh. But fearful? She'd never seen Simon afraid of anything.

"Listen," he tried and immediately petered out. Shook his head at himself and made a choking sound. Finally, he patted the floor beside him and whispered, "Sit." He looked up with beseeching eyes. "Please. Just sit. Listen. Please..."

She stared for a second, then took a step closer in spite of herself.

His voice was so quiet, so worn, she couldn't help but do as he said. She backed toward the stairs, not quite trusting, and lowered herself to the second one, keeping a height advantage over him for the tiny bit of confidence that brought.

"Listen, Jess..."

The way he said her name made her toes tingle, even though the rest of her fretted about what might come next. Some terrible revelation, some dark secret, maybe.

"You have to be careful, Jess. They're still out there."

Her mind raced, trying to remember what existed outside the four walls of the saloon. She'd been so preoccupied with Simon and work, she hadn't given anything else much thought.

"They're still out there..." His voice was hoarse, and a chill ran down her spine. "No one can know you're here. If Janna answers the phone like that, she's putting your life at risk. If they find out where you are..."

She didn't have to ask who *they* were. The rogues who called themselves Blue Bloods. The ones who'd murdered her family. The mad shifters who'd chanted as they watched her home burn.

Purity! Purity! No shifters shall mix! None shall taint shifter blood!

It was a miracle she and Janna had slipped away. But word must have gotten back to the rogues and their madman of a leader, Victor Whyte, because they'd hunted the sisters ever since. She and Janna had moved from one place to another, wondering where it would all end. And the first place she'd felt halfway secure was here. The wolves of Twin Moon pack were strong — so strong, that even out here on the fringes of their territory, a couple of packless she-wolves could feel reasonably safe. Couldn't they?

"No excuse to yell at my sister," she blurted, trying to hang on to the last scrap of her pride. "And anyway, what do you care?"

"I care," Simon barked. He didn't raise his voice, but the words still jolted her. "I care," he insisted. "I would die for you." His shoulders sagged with an unbearable burden, and his voice wavered. "I'd have done anything for you."

It was the truth he was choking on — his eyes said as much — and all she could do was stare.

"But you hate me."

He shook his head. "I don't hate you, Jess."

But he did. Didn't he?

"I just never knew how to explain," he said, so quietly, she nearly missed it.

"What is there to explain?"

He laughed bitterly. "Everything."

They sat for another minute, letting a heavy silence invade the room. Then Simon finally spoke — softly, barely chipping away at the edges of it.

"Remember what we promised?"

How could she forget? "We promised to work on convincing our families that an alliance would be a good thing. A blood alliance..." She trailed off there. She'd done her part. Why hadn't he done his?

"And we did it. We succeeded."

"Sure did," she said bitterly. Was he about to rub her face in his rejection again?

But Simon went on, gradually gathering speed. "The clan held a council meeting where my grandfather announced it. In front of everyone..."

She wondered why he sounded so bitter when that was supposed to be her job.

Simon's voice dropped an octave as he imitated his grandfather's scratchy voice. "I have spoken with the wolf pack, and they agree. The older Macks daughter—"

That was her. Did he have to drag the torture out so much?

"Shall be betrothed to one of our own clan. Voss blood, mixing with new blood." Simon paused and spoke in his own voice again. "Voss. Me! You know how happy I was?"

She remembered how happy she'd been when her father made the same announcement. And how hurt she'd been when Simon turned the cold shoulder.

"In three years, our clans shall come together again," Simon continued mimicking his grandfather's gritty tone. "To celebrate the mating of Jessica Macks and Soren Voss."

Jess was so consumed by bad memories, she'd have missed the punch line if Simon hadn't repeated it in his own growling tone. "Soren fucking Voss."

Her chin snapped up. "Soren?"

He grimaced. "Soren."

"But...but..."

"Yeah," he whispered. "That's what I said."

"So why didn't you do anything?"

"I did *everything*, Jess. I tried. But their minds were made up. Your parents', too. I tried talking to them, and you know what they said?"

Simon had had the guts to approach her parents after that?

"They said 'second son is second best,'" he grunted. "And second best wasn't good enough for you."

"But...but..." she mumbled it a couple of dozen times. "But I didn't want Soren!"

"Believe me, he didn't want you." Simon's hands shot up. "Wait, I mean, not like that. He found his own mate. He wanted her."

She stared at Simon. "Who?" Maybe if she focused on someone else, all this would be easier to grasp.

"Sarah Boone. Remember her?"

Barely. Soren was a few years older than her; Sarah, too. "Sarah, from the little shop in town?"

Simon nodded.

"Sarah, the human?" Jess gaped. "Holy..." She always thought she and Simon had their work cut out for them, convincing their shifter species to let them mate. But humans were totally off-limits. Then she gasped. "Sarah died..."

Simon shushed her with a harsh look at the doorway. "I know. He knows. They burned her alive. Burned the whole place down, just like they did with our clan and your pack."

They. The same evil *they.* Her stomach turned as she recalled the gleeful cries of the Blue Bloods drowning out the screams of her packmates. Remembered them growing fainter as she grabbed Janna and ran and ran and ran...

The shadows moved a little, and she shivered until she realized it was Simon, reaching a hand out. Did she dare take it?

The headlights of a passing car stabbed through the room, then drew away, and she found herself reaching for him. Winding her fingers through his and hanging on.

"I was stupid," Simon said. "So fucking stupid..."

Yes, you were, part of her wanted to snap. But now that she thought about it...

The bears have agreed to your betrothal to the Voss boy. That's all her father had said, and she'd assumed Simon, of course.

Maybe she'd been stupid, too. In all that time she'd put in, all the carefully worded lobbying to her father about the advantages of an alliance, she'd never mentioned Simon. Never dared mention Simon, because it was too early to admit that they were in love. Her pack was old-fashioned and needed time to swallow the idea of a wolf mating with a bear. But once they'd jumped on the idea, it had taken off like a runaway train.

And God, she'd been ignorant of the truth this whole time.

His breath came in uneven rasps, and she was about to speak when a voice came from the hallway, making them both look up.

"Simon?"

It was Soren. Nowhere near as ferocious as before, but curt enough to drag them out of their thoughts.

Simon looked at her. Squeezed her hand. Pulled it closer until he had it pressed against his chest.

Her eyes slid shut. That contact was her anchor. Her hope. Her one chance not to lose it completely while she tried to process everything he'd said.

"Simon," Soren called again.

Simon sighed wearily and called quietly back. "Be right there."

He pushed himself to his feet and held a hand out, helping her to her feet. God, she felt a hundred years older, but none the wiser.

"There's so much more I have to say," he whispered.

She nodded mutely. Yes, there was. But what she'd just heard was overwhelming enough. A minute or two — better yet, a week or two — to catch up with her racing emotions probably wouldn't hurt.

"Simon," Soren called.

She blinked at the hallway. Soren, she wasn't quite ready to face. Soren, the man her family wanted to marry her off to instead of the man she loved.

It made sense, in a convoluted, barbarian way. She was the eldest Macks child. Soren was the eldest Voss, the one poised to take over the clan someday. Bringing their families together would be a win-win. But Christ, hadn't anyone bothered to ask her? To even tell her?

God, if her parents were alive, she'd have marched right over and given them a piece of her mind. But they were dead, and she couldn't summon any anger any more. Only bewilderment.

Jesus, she couldn't even imagine being mated to Soren. She'd never, ever wanted anyone but Simon. Never.

Second son, second best? Her grandmother used to joke that about a cousin's marriage into another pack. Jess had never linked it to Simon, though. To her, he was always the best. The only.

Simon stepped away. She didn't even notice his hand was still wrapped around hers until it slipped out, and then the absence was striking. Painful, almost.

"I have to go out," Soren said as Simon drew near, and they both turned down the hall.

She hung back in the shadows, not ready to face Soren just yet. She detoured to the ladies' room. Maybe she could get herself together again.

She stared at herself in the mirror.

Yeah, right.

Chapter Ten

Simon watched the saloon doors swing on their hinges long after his brother left, off for a late-night meeting at Twin Moon Ranch.

"You okay here?" Soren had asked. "I have to get going."

Not really okay, but...sure. He'd keep an eye on things, all right.

Harry and most of the customers were gone. Cole was hanging back to wait for Janna, who pranced right over to Jess the minute she emerged from the back, blinking like a deer in headlights. Straight as a ramrod, too, because Jess was tough and strong, even after being slapped with a revelation like that. That her family was ready to marry her off to the wrong man. That she was still being hunted by the rogues. It was a wonder she didn't crumple to the ground and refuse to go on.

Not Jess. Not my Jess, his bear chuffed in pride.

No, not his Jess. But Christ, it would be nice if she didn't have to be so damn tough.

"Are you okay?" Janna asked.

He could see Jessica's eyes flutter about before she answered with a terse, "Fine."

He let out a little snort. She was about as fine as he was.

"Listen, I was going to go dancing. You okay with that?" Janna asked.

Jessica's head snapped toward the door in alarm, and he could read her thoughts. *Rogues. Closing in. Hunting...*

"Some of the guys from the ranch invited me out," Janna said. She leaned in and whispered the rest. "And Cole is coming, too."

Simon looked out the front windows, where a couple of trucks were parked, surrounded by three ranch hands. Wolves — big, hardy wolves toughened by hard work and the sun. Ty wasn't kidding when he said he'd send someone over to keep an eye on things.

Jess glanced over at him, and he gave a curt nod. Honest shifters from an honest pack were nothing to worry about. Neither was Cole. Janna would be fine.

"Um...sure," Jess said. "Have fun."

Knowing Janna, she would.

"I'll do the cleanup next time," Janna promised and headed for the door, where Cole was waiting.

A second later, trucks started up outside and drove away, and Simon and Jess spent a long minute staring at each other, not knowing where to start.

"You sure she'll be okay?" Jess asked.

"The guys will keep an eye on Janna," he said. *And I'll keep an eye on you.*

She stared for a moment, as if she'd read his thoughts. Then she shook herself a little and sputtered into the next sentence. "You think that Cole is an okay guy?"

He shrugged. "Seems like a decent guy. He has no clue about shifters, but with the rest of the guys around...Janna will be fine."

"Good," Jess mumbled. "What about Soren? Where did he go?"

"He had a meeting at the ranch."

Just you and me left, his bear rumbled inside. *Just you and me.*

Her eyes widened. She gulped. Her nostrils flared.

And just when Simon thought she might say something to jump-start the conversation they had to finish, she swung into action. "Got to clean up."

And zoom, she was off, headed for the kitchen.

"Jess. . . " he tried, but she immediately shook her head.

He sighed and watched her disappear, then eventually reappear with cleaning supplies.

"Gotta clean up. . . "

She murmured the words like a mantra, so he backed off. Maybe now wasn't the time to push an off-kilter she-wolf. Even he had enough sense to know that. If cleaning and numbering and organizing helped her feel together, he'd let her go at it.

So he dragged out a dishcloth and started closing down the bar, peeking at her from the corner of his eye. She wiped every table twice. Some of them, three times. Rearranged the salt and pepper shakers until they were angled exactly right. Nudged the tables into place until she was satisfied, then headed out for the mop.

He sighed and started flipping chairs, which brought her to a sharp stop when she came back.

He raised his eyebrows in challenge. *Yes, I'm stacking chairs for you. Yes, I love you. No, I never stopped.*

She scurried to the corner where the pool table stood, turned her back, and let the wet slap of the mop do the talking. *Not ready. So not ready. I still hate you...I think.*

Of course, she didn't hate him. But he'd hurt her, badly, and she wasn't ready to forgive.

He rolled down the metal gate that covered the swinging saloon doors, then closed the inner door, and locked everything for the night. He checked them twice before going back to the bar to finish up there.

And on it went, the two of them dancing around the silence that hung between them. They were champs at awkward avoidance by now. Why not keep it up?

When the phone rang, they both jumped and stared. Eventually, Simon picked it up.

"Hello?" he barked.

"Simon?" came the voice at the end of the line.

Not a rogue. A familiar voice. "Kyle?"

"Listen, can you come out and help?" The urgency in Kyle's voice made him stand straighter. Kyle Williams, wolf shifter and Arizona state cop. Twin Moon pack's inside man in local law enforcement.

"What's up?"

Jessica cocked her head, listening.

"You got that she-wolf with you?" Kyle asked.

Every nerve in his body went on red alert. Jess had heard, too; he saw her hands go white around the mop handle.

"Simon!" Kyle half-shouted. "Is she with you?"

"Yes," he admitted, locking eyes with Jess. If they could trust anyone, they could trust Kyle.

"Good. Bring her. We need every nose we can get."

Chapter Eleven

"Which one is Kyle?" Jess asked, sliding out of Simon's car, still thinking about everything Simon had said on the drive over.

Please. Just sit. Listen...

I never knew how to explain...

Second son is second best...

What hell had he been living in all these years?

"Tall guy, spiky hair. Cop uniform." Simon pointed to a handful of people huddled in the headlights of a vehicle in the state park lot, but his shoulders still had that uncharacteristic slump.

Stupid. I was so fucking stupid...

God, how long had he been beating himself up over what he'd had to do?

She stopped dead in her tracks and looked up, sniffing. Was that smoke in the air?

Her nostrils flared. Definitely smoke. But with the breeze blowing from behind her, it was hard to ascertain how near or how far the fire was. How big.

She shuddered and rubbed her hands over her arms.

Simon noticed, too; he tilted his chin up to sniff. But his eyes were intent on the people ahead. "Come on. Kyle wouldn't have called if it wasn't important."

"Cop?" she asked nervously. There were good cops, and there were bad cops. "Why does he need us? Why does he need me?"

Simon put a hand on her shoulder, and damn it, her wolf calmed right down. The beast had been sniffing and yowling for him on the twenty-minute drive out of town. She glanced up and cursed the three-quarter full moon for the tenth time that evening. No wonder her wolf was so close to the surface tonight. And it would only get worse in the coming days as the moon grew fuller.

"He's one of us," Simon whispered.

A shifter? She didn't dare ask. Didn't need to once they'd gotten close enough for her to clearly identify the one shifter by his telltale scent. No human would ever pick up on it, but a fellow wolf sure could. Kyle was tall, with spiky hair, just as Simon had said, and his brow was furrowed in deep rows. He nodded at her and Simon in a quiet greeting.

"The child was last seen in Sunrise Campground five hours ago," a uniformed woman said.

Jessica's mind exploded with alarms. A child? Lost?

That's when she heard the sobbing coming from the right. A woman was hunched at a picnic table, surrounded by two or three others trying to console her. "My baby! Oh my God! Laurel!" She rocked back and forth, crying into her hands.

The police went on with their brief, the very picture of cool and calm. Their brows were furrowed, though, their jaws tense.

"Which means," the female officer said, "the girl could be anywhere within this radius." She drew a red circle on a map spread on the hood of a car.

"We've got state police searching this quadrant." Kyle's hand waved over the map. "And a couple of National Guard volunteers over here."

"Oh God, oh God..." the mother wailed in the background. The sound tore the edges of Jessica's heart.

"Under no circumstances are you to head north and approach the perimeter of the fire," Kyle said.

Fire. Jess looked up as her blood ran cold. *Please, not a forest fire. Not tonight.*

An owl hooted from a stand of cottonwoods marking the head of the trail.

"You're to search the western slopes only," Kyle said firmly to the volunteers gathered around. "Coconino, Pine, and Pinyon trails. Circle around, then check back here."

Everyone ducked to check out the map except Kyle, Simon, and Jess. The cop-shifter's eyes met theirs in a clear message. *You follow your noses, wherever they lead you.*

Simon gave a tiny nod and looked up, his nose twitching. Facing north, the direction of the fire.

Jess forced herself to breathe evenly. This was about a lost child, not about her and Simon, or her own fears.

Kyle turned back to the others. "The time is currently 11:25 p.m. I want everyone back in ninety minutes. There's no telling which way that fire might go."

"Cell phone reception in the park is spotty, but just in case..." The female officer dictated a number as Simon led Jess quietly toward where the mother sat.

"I checked the tent, and she was gone," the mother was crying. "I should have checked earlier. I should have checked..."

Jessica's eyes went straight to the woman, but Simon's were in her lap. "That her teddy bear?" he asked.

His voice was gruff as ever, but gentle, too. Gentle enough for the mother to look up through her tears and hold the toy up.

"Yes," she whispered, then collapsed into sobs again. "Oh God..."

Simon grabbed Jessica's hand and pulled her toward the trailhead for Sunrise Trail. He took off, taking long, swinging paces up the trail. Jessica's steps were shorter, but she glided along behind him with her quick, efficient stride.

"You got the scent?" he asked, just as a bat fluttered over their heads.

Jess threw a hand up as it whooshed overhead and plowed on.

"Got it."

The woman had held the teddy bear up long enough for both of them to get a whiff, thank goodness. And a whiff was all they needed. Even in human form, Jessica's sense of smell was much more sensitive than any human's. And bears had the best noses on the planet. If anyone could find that child, they would.

She balled her hands into fists, picturing the mother's anguish. Picturing the child, lost and afraid. They had to find that little girl. They had to!

Pale moonlight trickled past the branches of the trees, casting shadows that shifted and slid as she strode past.

"Jesus, why was that family camping when there is a fire?"

Simon didn't look back. "The fire just broke out. The whole valley's been too dry. All it takes is one spark, one cigarette..."

84

It might have been something as innocuous as that, but Jess couldn't help picturing a dozen crazed rogues, throwing fuel on a fire. Circling her homestead to block anyone's escape. Chanting into the night.

Purity! Purity!

She caught a shiver before it got too far down her back. This was not about that awful night. This was about that little girl. And fire or no fire, she'd get the kid out, just as she'd gotten Janna out of the inferno in Montana.

She sniffed as she walked, trying to match something with the buttercup-and-baby-shampoo scent she'd picked up from the teddy bear, but there were too many competing scents on this part of the trail. The scent of hikers, fresh and sweaty, young and old. Someone had tossed a rotting apple not far from the trail, and a deer had brushed by not too long ago. A dog had run zigzags across the trail, too, hours ago. She couldn't see much in the shadows, but her nose caught it all.

She walked as fast as she could without breaking into a trot, because that threatened to bring the panic out. Simon seemed to sense it, too, and kept his pace in check.

"You good?" he murmured thirty minutes later, cresting a rise just ahead of her.

"I'm goo—"

She stopped cold, taking in the sight ahead. A valley fell away before them and a pine-dotted hillside rose on the other side. All was quiet there, but behind it, a higher ridge stood out, covered in flames.

"Jesus," she whispered. The whole forest was on fire.

She jumped when the bushes rustled. A rabbit shot past, then a deer. She could feel their urgency, their fear. Could feel her own fear, welling up.

"You good?" Simon repeated, stepping closer.

Mate. Focus on our mate, her wolf said inside.

He's not our mate, she wanted to protest, but she couldn't summon the willpower. Simon's voice was her anchor, her keel. Her light.

"I'm good." She nodded.

He studied her for a second, then took off downhill. Into the valley. Closer to the fire.

The air grew heavy as they descended. A thin layer of smoke crept over the landscape, filling the lowest contours of the valley. But the scent of the little girl grew stronger, too.

Simon kicked at the ground around an abandoned tent then headed upslope again. Jessica veered away from him, following a different trail, until they met again a few steps later.

"Okay, so she went in circles for a while..." Jess started.

Simon growled and they both circled again, moving more urgently all the time.

"Here!" she shouted, finally locating a trail that led away from the campsite.

Simon loped over, and they both set off again. Jess tried keeping the child's scent in the forefront of her mind, but the fresher scent of smoke was overpowering everything, throwing her concentration off.

"I'm losing it," she cried in frustration.

"I got it." His voice was a gruff, let-me-focus tone.

Bear noses were keener than wolves. Keener than a bloodhound's. But could he track through the thickening smoke?

"Stop!" Jess shouted a few minutes later, and both of them held absolutely still. "I heard something!"

A faint, crackling sound, like a person crawling through the undergrowth.

"Shit." She drooped. It was only the sound of the fire consuming the woods.

Simon plunged ahead, then stopped, pulled his shirt off, and threw it at her. What the hell was he doing?

He cursed. "I'm losing the scent, too." He shucked his pants, too, then his briefs, and she had a wide-eyed look at all the parts of Simon she hadn't seen for far, far too long before he bent over with a low huff.

He fell to the ground and landed on all fours. His back curved and darkened with hair. Short, thick strands that quickly became fur, exactly the color of his sandy brown hair. His rear dipped and rounded into haunches, and when he swung his head around...

Jess caught a breath. Her bear. Her mighty, fearless bear.

"Simon..." she whispered.

The scent of him pushed everything else away. All the worry, the nightmares, the doubt. The scent of Simon the man wafted from the clothes bundled in her arms, and the scent of Simon the bear drifted to her from two steps away. The scent of her past.

God, she'd loved him so much.

God, she still did.

His head dipped and he murmured a mournful syllable, blinking at her.

God, I love you, his dark eyes said. At least, they seemed to. And for the first time ever, she was tempted to break down the barriers she'd erected around her mind. Tempted to let his thoughts in and share hers in return.

A bird of prey whistled, soaring overhead, and both of them whipped their heads around. The flames were licking over the ridgeline now, the fire rumbling ahead.

"Go," she whispered. "Go."

Simon studied her for another second, then blinked. He let his nose lead his body in a wide arc, chuffed once, and took off again.

Jess stood rooted for a moment, mesmerized by his flowing bear gait. Then she snapped into action, too. She balanced his clothes atop a boulder and took off after him on two feet. No use in shifting into wolf form right now. Simon had the scent, and if they did find the child, she'd be the one to grab it.

Not if. When. When we find the child. She told herself that again and again as she ran up the hill behind her bear. *We. We...*

The *we* was the only part of the situation she liked. That, and the part about *her* bear. God, if they made it down the mountain alive, they'd have a lot of talking to do.

Her panting breaths turned to coughs as the smoke grew thicker, the fire louder. Up and up and up they ran, with Simon slaloming left and right, following an invisible trail. How he could pick up anything but the fire was beyond her. He ran on even when the treetops above them crackled in the intense heat. He ran on as the pines all around erupted in flames. He ran on, barely flinching when a towering pine groaned and crashed to the ground in an eerie, slow-motion way.

"Simon!" she screamed, squinting through the smoke.

He glanced back and grunted at her to turn back.

Her cry turned into a curse. Like hell, she'd turn back now. She leaped over a burning branch and followed him through the trees, straight at a wall of fire no sane creature would approach.

Simon paced the fireline, roaring his frustration into the flames. The fire teased and taunted him with strands that darted out then danced away. He paced left; Jess ran up behind him and paced right, ready to scream into the night. Where was the child?

"Laurel!" she yelled.

The fire laughed back.

"Laurel!" she tried again, running along the slope. "Laurel!"

Simon set off in the opposite direction, roaring into the night.

Jess ran another few steps, bounded over a log, then stopped and whipped around.

"Laurel?" She called softly. Too softly, really, to be heard above the flames.

Her ears twitched at the sound of a scratch. A sniff.

"Laurel!" Jess ran back around the log, looking frantically around. "Lau—"

She looked upslope and caught the tiniest movement. Something small and bright. Yellow cloth. Yellow pajamas?

"Simon!" She ran forward, then promptly retreated. Two fallen trees were burning in a vee-shape that pointed her way, forming a barrier.

Again, the movement — and a whimper.

Jess shoved at the end of one tree. It was hot but not burning at the end nearest her — yet. Even shoving with all her might didn't budge it, though. She screamed her frustration into the night. "Simon!"

The breath it took to yell forced her to inhale, and she folded over, heaving and coughing, on the cusp of defeat.

The earth shook. A huge, bristling shape rocketed past her and thumped into the tree.

She looked through a curtain of tears, through the smoke. Simon.

He roared at the tree. Bulldozed it along the ground, sending crackling flames flying. He pushed it upslope and out of the way, only for it to roll back.

Simon bellowed, braced his legs, and pushed again. The tree shifted and rolled closer, but a tiny gap opened up.

Get her! Get her! Simon's roar said.

Jess darted through the gap Simon barely held open. She jumped a line of fire that reached for her in midair, stumbled to a stop, and looked down. A round face darkened with soot and a pair of wide, beseeching eyes shone at her from a hollow.

"Laurel!" Jess yelped.

She snatched the child up and jumped back over the burning branch. Cut left, then right, around the only patch of ground free of flames, and leaped for her life. The tree thundered back into place, closing the gap behind her with an angry shower of sparks. Simon was nowhere to be seen, and a second log started rolling downhill behind her.

There was no time to think. No time to scream for Simon. All she could do was run for her life and the child's. She ran in bounding kangaroo steps down the slope and prayed as she went.

The woods behind her hissed as the rolling log hit a tree and careened to a stop, shooting a hailstorm of sparks her way.

She didn't stop to look. Just tugged the fabric of her shirt up, hid the little girl's face in it, and ran on. Two thin hands clutched at her back; two thin legs bounced against her hip as she ran and ran and ran.

God, where was Simon? Where was he?

She raced across the bottom of the valley and up the other side, crying for Simon in her mind. Her lungs screamed for clean air as she pounded uphill, toward safety, and when she reached the top, she looked back, hugging the whimpering child.

"It will be okay. Everything will be okay," she whispered. The words were as much for herself as for the child, because where was Simon? God, where was he?

A helicopter zipped overhead, circled, and cast a curtain of water across the hill. Flames and shadows danced everywhere. Any one of them could have been a bear or a man. Her eyes darted back and forth. God, where was Simon?

"Mommy..." the little girl cried.

Jess clutched her closer to her aching heart. "It will be okay..."

Her fist rose in a triumph a moment later. "Simon!"

There he was, running up the hill. Stark-naked, in human form, with his clothes bundled under his arm.

Jess hunched over the little girl and let herself shed a few tears before turning for the way out. Within a few strides, she was back to a jog with Simon racing up behind.

She didn't want to look his way. Didn't trust herself to. But her head turned of its own volition, and there he was. He'd gotten his jeans on but not the shirt, and his whole torso was streaked with soot. A black smudge ran down one cheek where he'd wiped away his sweat, and his hair stuck up wildly, like he'd been electrified.

Electrified. A little like she felt, seeing him alive.

"You good?" he murmured, as if they were simply hiking down a mountain and not racing for their lives.

She laughed, tiptoeing the fine line between control and hysteria, and ran on. Even without death nipping at her heels, she refused to slow down. The minute she did, she suspected, she'd be a nervous wreck. Nightmares tugged at her sleeve as she went, trying to remind her of another night, another fire.

"Mommy!"

"Laurel!"

Jess blinked as the girl was torn from her arms and voices sounded all around. In surprise. In joy. In relief.

"Are you all right?"

"Breathe easy..."

"Holy shit..."

A camera flashed. Booted feet rushed by.

"All right, now," the female police officer said. "Everyone back up."

She bent at the waist and heaved for all the air she'd done without on the run down. Hands tapped at her shoulders, but she ignored them all — except one. The one she knew, somehow just knew, was Simon's. That hand she clutched at and refused to let go.

Chapter Twelve

Simon blinked into headlights. The whole parking lot was lit up like command central. Fire trucks had arrived on the scene, and people scurried back and forth. Some slapped him on the back, others urged him out of the way. He guided Jessica to one side of the bustle, keeping his eyes locked on her.

They'd done it. Jesus. They'd done it.

He held on to her hand, tipped his head back, and tried to pick the stars out of the sky beyond the glare of the lights. Slowly, his vision adjusted and the stars peeked out, one by one. He winced in anticipation of a faint note of scorn from the universe. For the past six months, it had been that way. He'd search for some sign, some hint of acceptance, but all he ever got was the cold shoulder.

But this time, the stars winked and smiled. He looked for Ursa Major, the Great Bear, the constellation that had always guided his clan. And damned if those stars weren't shining on him the brightest of all. Practically patting him on the back for the long, hard road he'd traveled.

Jesus, they'd done it.

He'd done it.

He bent over Jess and ran a hand over her back, trying

to soothe her the way she'd soothed the child. *It'll be okay. Everything will be okay.*

Somehow, everything would.

Kyle came up and clamped a hand on Simon's shoulder longer than he had to. "Good job, man. Good job."

He managed a grin, then pointed at Jess.

The cop cracked into a huge smile and leaned closer. "The real hero, huh? Our women always are."

Our women. The women of Twin Moon pack. Yeah, they had a reputation for that.

Simon straightened and subtly stepped between Kyle and Jess. She may have been a ward of Twin Moon pack, but first and foremost, she was part of *his* clan.

Mine, his bear chuffed with pride. *Mine.*

Kyle's gaze danced between the two of them, and he promptly backed off. "I get it. Believe me, I get it." He grinned. A full, happy grin the cop so rarely showed. "Now get her out of here and take her home."

Home. Simon liked the sound of that. And the image that came with it: not the thick woods of Montana, but the apartment over the saloon. His saloon.

But there were grateful parents to meet and police questions to answer. Jess handled it like a champ, even though she had to be nearing the end of her rope. She patted the little girl, spoke to her again. So calm and soothing that his bear got all warm and fuzzy inside. She even flashed him a smile. *We did it. We got her. She's safe.*

He soared like an eagle, just on the strength of that smile.

When he got Jess into the truck and drove off, his bear felt more settled than he had in years. But Jess... Her lips zipped, her shoulders sagged. Well, it had been a hell of a night. A hell of a morning, in fact, coming on two a.m.

She reached for his hand and hung on to it for most of the drive. Whenever he changed gears, she'd let go briefly, then clamp down over him again. Like he was a comfort to her. Like he made her feel safe. His bear had hummed with the sheer joy of it. Hell, he could have driven all the way to Mexico if she'd kept that up.

But when they'd gotten within sight of the saloon, Jess abruptly let go. They had scarcely pulled into the parking lot behind the saloon when she bolted out of the truck. She slammed the door behind her, rushed into the building, and ran up the stairs.

Simon stayed in the driver's seat for a good, long while, wondering what the hell was up. Was she worried about her sister seeing them together? About Soren being back? But the lights were all off; everyone else was still out.

He stared into the darkness for a while. Maybe it was him. Maybe he'd messed up again.

Inside. Find mate. Now! his bear demanded.

He slid out of the truck and closed the door slowly in case slamming it spooked her. He walked up the stairs to the apartment as quietly as he could, though there wasn't much point on those creaky stairs. Headed down the hallway as far as his room and stopped by the plant in the corner. One of several plants she and Janna had set around the place. He sniffed. Listened. Sensed.

Home, his bear hummed. *Home.*

He paused there, processing that. Over the past few weeks, he'd never looked around much when he headed upstairs and went to bed. No thinking, not much looking around besides the longing sniffs in her direction. But now, he noticed. The plant, for starters. A big, leafy one, almost as tall as him. The braided rug on the floor. When had that gotten there?

Home. His bear nodded in satisfaction. *Home.*

Another plant stood in the far corner, and the two of them brought a touch of the outdoors into the place. Maybe that's what made his bear feel settled.

But not entirely settled, because he had to check on his mate.

Mate. His bear nodded firmly. *Mine.*

He tiptoed toward the corner where the hallway turned ninety degrees in the direction of Jessica's room. A corner he'd turned a thousand times in dusky dreams but never in real life.

She needs us. Hurry up.

He stepped a little faster. Did she really need him? Did she really want him?

Yes, the scent of her, lingering in the hallway, said. *Yes.*

He paused at the next corner, having come nearly full circle around the apartment, and hesitated on the border to her forbidden realm. But when he heard her sniffling not far ahead, he just about ran the rest of the way. He threw a hand out to brake himself on the doorway and gulped.

"Jess?"

She stood facing the window, peering out toward the burning hills. Trembling. Knotting her fingers around each other and twisting them again and again.

"Jess, are you okay?"

"Fine," she mumbled.

Not fine, his bear decided. *Not fine at all.*

He eased into the room, one careful step at a time, and when she didn't protest, he slid an arm over her shoulders. She was as smudged and sooty as he was, but who cared? He reached his other arm around her front and waited for her to protest.

She leaned the slightest, tiniest bit his way, then crumpled into his arms, and he hugged her close. Hugged her with everything he had and mumbled and ran a hand over her hair.

"It's okay," he whispered as she cried softly, her tears soaking his shirt. "It's okay." His heart was bursting with conflicting emotions. Joy, from being able to touch her again. Distress, at witnessing his mate's sorrow.

"It was just like that," she mumbled again and again.

Just like what?

"Just like that night..."

For the first time in years, he dared reach his thoughts out toward hers. It used to be they could whisper to each other without uttering a sound. They could send thoughts into each other's minds, until they'd both thrown up brick walls. But tonight...maybe...

He reached his mind toward hers and winced at what he saw. A forest at night, aflame.

"It was just like that..."

Screams. Howls. Some of agony, others of glee.

Jess pressed her hands over her ears, reliving the sounds. "Stop. Stop. Run away."

She didn't mean him. She meant the shadowy fig-ures throwing diesel on the fire and reveling as the flames licked higher. She meant Janna, whose hand was shaking in Jessica's, at least in her memories.

"Jess. It's okay." He squeezed just hard enough to chase that awful night away.

"It was the same. Me and Janna, rushing through the forest. Wondering who was out there. Trying to get away..."

She shook and blabbered a little, and her wolf howled inside. Everything he'd missed at Black River, she'd had to suffer through.

"All my fault..." she mumbled.

He pulled away and took her by both shoulders. "It wasn't your fault, Jess. How could it be your fault?"

"They all died. Everyone but Janna and me."

He shook his head vehemently. "The rogues did that, not you. Jess, it wasn't you."

"My fault, because I pushed my pack to get closer to your clan. I pushed for the alliance through our mating." Tears seeped through his shirt and she clutched harder.

"No," he said. "No." He'd been down that rabbit hole himself, but it wasn't true. He'd screwed a lot of things up, but not that. Not loving her. "That was the rogues. The rogues killed your family."

"I brought it on them."

He shook her slightly. "Love, Jess. It was love. How could that be a bad thing?"

She stared at him. Her lip trembled.

His heart pounded. The blood in his veins roared. *Say it! Say it again!*

"I loved you. I still love you. And nothing — nothing — will ever make that wrong."

She gaped, probably because he was nearly shouting, but he couldn't help it. He'd accept responsibility for lots of fucking up. For hurting her, too. But he'd never, ever regret loving her. Not for one instant.

"Our love didn't kill anyone," he insisted. "The rogues did. Don't mix it up, Jess. Don't."

She clutched his shoulders and looked at him through teary eyes. "But what about now? It's all messed up."

Where his answer came from, he didn't know. From a well of wisdom he didn't know he had, maybe? From all the ghosts of his past? "Doesn't have to be. Doesn't have to be."

She searched his eyes, so he plunged on.

"Destiny wanted us together. We have our chance now. We can take it." The words just poured out of him. Out of his heart, out of his soul.

"Destiny..." she echoed uncertainly.

"Destiny." He nodded. "How did you even get here? To Arizona, I mean?"

"I don't know. I just... I just followed..."

He knew exactly what she meant. That pull, that inner compass saying, *Come here. You need to come here.*

"You followed instinct, right?"

She nodded. "Janna and I were hitchhiking, and it felt like..." She motioned vaguely while she groped for words.

"Like that kids' game, playing hot and cold. Getting warmer, warmer... Right?"

"Right. It just felt right. But then it felt like we'd gone too far, so we got the driver to drop us off."

"Where?" He held his breath. "Where?"

She stared at him. "Here. Not a block away from here. We were asking around for jobs, and one of the ranch hands sniffed us out and brought us to Tina..."

He nodded her along.

"And she took us back to the ranch. Even offered us a place to stay there, but..."

"But?" It felt as if his future hung on that word.

"But it didn't *feel* right. So we asked her about something else..."

A long, relieved breath left him. He and Soren had done close to the same thing.

"She brought me to you," Jess whispered. She stroked his shoulder gently. Almost hopefully.

"Destiny brought you here," he said, finally certain of one thing. "Destiny brought us together again."

He pulled her into another hug and hung on and on, because he finally understood. All the doubt, the pain, the hopelessness — it wasn't for nothing. It had all been worthwhile, because it brought him back to his mate.

"You know what Soren and I did?" Now he was the one blabbering, but what did that matter? "We hunted every last rogue we could find. Killed every one that had been in Montana, down to the last one. And then we were done. Empty. Spent. Never felt so empty in my life. We dug a den and crawled into it..." He trailed off, choking on the thought, then forced himself to go on. She'd said her part; he'd say his. "We crawled in to die because we thought our mates were dead. Lay there for a week, waiting for it..."

She ran her hands over his back. "No! Simon! No."

He shook his head. "But it didn't work. My bear wouldn't let go. And I thought I was a worse failure because of it."

"What?" She pulled back. "How could you?"

"Not only did I fail my clan, I couldn't even die like I should have. The way the old stories say. That when one mate dies..."

"...the other follows," she finished. "They give up on life to follow their mate."

100

He nodded. "And I couldn't even do that right. But it wasn't that..." God, now he understood. "My bear wouldn't let go because you were still alive. You were still out there..."

"Looking for you," she said.

Now it was his turn to stare. "Looking for me?"

She wiped the tears from her eyes and stood a little straighter. "I was looking for something. I didn't know what. But it was you. I was looking for you."

"You..." Even his bear was trembling inside. *Looking for me?*

"I love you," she whispered once, then said it louder. "I love you. Even when you didn't love me—"

He winced. "I always loved you. I'm so, so sorry about the rest."

Say it again, idiot, his bear demanded. *Say both those things a thousand times.*

He tried, but he couldn't, because her eyes flashed and her hands tightened on his shirt.

"I'm sor—" he started, but he didn't finish because she pulled him closer and covered his mouth with hers in a kiss. A kiss that knocked the wind out of him, it felt that good.

"Maybe it's time we both stopped being sorry," she said when she came up for air. "Maybe it's time we just let ourselves live."

He tried to say something, even if he had no clue what that might be. But then it didn't matter any more, because she kissed him again. She nudged the length of her body along the length of his and ignited a whole different fire inside.

Chapter Thirteen

Jess closed her eyes and focused everything on the kiss. Just as she had in the forest, when she'd shut everything out to follow her nose. Except this time, she was following her soul, and her soul led to him.

To Simon. Her Simon. Her bear.

Maybe seeing him in bear form did it. Maybe it was the fact that she'd kept her wolf locked away for so long. She didn't know which — only that she needed him. Wanted him. Loved him.

She took a deep breath between kisses and said it out loud. "I need you. I want you. I love you."

Simon's lips trembled. He didn't speak, but his thoughts shot straight into her mind. *I love you.* He cupped her face in both hands and looked her in the eye. *Never stopped. Never will.*

He leaned forward, pushing her back against the wall. Simon tilted his head and fit his lips over hers as only he could. His lips were dry on the outside, soft on the inside, like the honey on the edge of a honey jar and the amber liquid within. His tongue moved like honey, too, slow and steady and sweet, and his fingers threaded into her hair.

When he pulled back, it was with a sureness and serenity she hadn't seen since she'd first stepped foot in the saloon. And she felt it, too. Sure. Serene.

The left corner of his mouth twitched. His hands tightened around her waist as his eyes narrowed on her lips. She wrapped her arms around his neck and hauled him in. She hauled in a deep breath, too, because she knew she'd need it for this kiss.

A blink of the eye later, he had her hard against the wall. Hard against his body. Hard in every way, except for his lips, which started moving over hers. But when she whimpered and wrapped her leg around his, his kisses grew hotter, deeper. Needier.

His tongue swept the corners of her mouth. His fingers knotted in her hair, tilting her head right. His heart pounded against hers, and all the time his bear chanted into her mind.

This is mine, the bear puffed. *You are mine.*

She whimpered for more, burning up in the best possible way. Clearing her mind of everything but the solid wall of muscle under her hands.

Safe, his bear rumbled to her wolf. *Will always keep you safe.*

If she'd been in animal form, she'd have flicked her tail and licked his face. It had been so long. Six months of running. Three years of missing him. A lifetime of wishing.

"Simon..." She clutched his shirt — his dusty, sooty shirt — and wrestled it over that thick chest. Fought it over those round shoulders. Then she stopped, trapping his hands. She stroked his cheeks with her thumbs.

"What are you doing, my little she-wolf?" he whispered.

"Touching you." She circled his ears, traced the bridge of his nose. Testing him, maybe. Would his bear trust her even when she had him wrapped up like that?

His mouth curled into an indulgent smile. "Then touch. Take. Tickle. Whatever you want."

She grinned a little, picturing how a tickle might go. He'd have her hog-tied in her own shirt in two seconds flat if she tried that. Which didn't sound too bad, but her lips were greedy for another kiss.

More, her wolf begged. *More.*

She pulled the shirt off and threw it aside.

He blinked like a bear emerging from a den into sunshine with eyes that said *she* was his sunshine.

"Now you," he rumbled, tugging the hem of her shirt.

Her ash-covered, smoky shirt. The second she became aware of it, she wanted it gone. But he put his hands over hers and made her do it slowly. Dragged his hands over every inch of her curves, while his eyes glowed brighter and brighter.

Mine, his bear sang into her mind. *This is mine.*

He was marking her. Claiming her. Branding her with his touch.

She inhaled, letting her chest expand into his hands.

The shirt fluttered over her head and joined his somewhere across the room. Almost in a different universe. He didn't tease her with it the way she'd teased him, but the second his eyes focused on her bra, she knew he'd take his revenge.

"Pretty." His voice was husky as he ran a finger along the edge of the black lace.

"You like?" She coaxed him closer.

He nodded and traced the underside with his thumbs. "I like."

He reached all the way around the back, and she thought he'd free her of it at last. But he just growled under his breath and went right on circling the edges, torturing her. "I like."

"Then touch. Take, damn it. Tickle, if you like." She said it breathlessly, almost pleading for relief. The heat inside her body all rushed to her core, and her wolf begged for more.

His fingers twitched against her skin, and he hummed. "Soon. Very soon."

He nuzzled her chin, then her neck as his thumbs continued their long, even strokes. His fingers slid over the cups of her bra, teasing more than tickling. Then they dragged across the silk and pressed down on her nipples as she writhed under his touch.

"Simon, please..."

The kiss he planted on her collarbone turned into a nip, then a suck. A diversion, as it turned out, because a second later, he had the bra strap over her shoulder. The right cup hung loose.

"My, my," he growled. "What does my perfect she-wolf have here?" His lips followed his eyes toward the soft flesh of her breast.

My wolf. A week ago, she'd have whacked him over the head for that. Now, it made her soul sing.

My bear! My man! My mate!

She tipped her head right and watched him dip lower, lower. Thick fingers explored the inside of the cup.

"You're supposed to be touching me, not the bra."

"Ah, but I like this bra. I like...touching...it." He turned his fingers as he spoke the last two words and slid them over her skin.

She inhaled sharply, trying to keep her lusty wolf under control.

"So touch some more."

Her knees wobbled under her, and just like that, he lowered her to the mattress. So smoothly, so seamlessly, she barely noticed until she was flat on her back and sinking into it.

"Okay?" he whispered.

"Perfect. Beautiful," she mumbled, tugging his head into place.

The bra strap was down by her elbow, and he flipped the cup down. He took her breast easily in his mitt of a hand and toyed with it. Teased the nipple until it stood out like a button, then smoothed it over and started again, murmuring, "Perfect. Beautiful..."

In one long, hot drag, he sanded his chin down her flesh and kissed. Licked. Rubbed with his stubble, then soothed with his tongue until she was totally, utterly on fire.

"Yes..." she moaned.

His mouth worked her hard — almost painfully hard — but even that didn't seem like enough.

She was barely aware of him working the button of her jeans, pushing them down. Guiding her feet out of them and her panties, and she only vaguely registered lying naked but for the bra.

Until his fingers started exploring, that is.

He kneeled over her, suckling at her breast, twisting and nipping and rubbing one side on the skin, the other through the silk. Broad fingers slid up her legs, then down, guiding her legs apart while his other hand discarded her bra. Up and down, in a long line from her knee to her hip. Then the curve of her thigh, and then between.

"Simon..." she murmured as he traced her folds.

He spread his palm over her, too wide to penetrate, and let it dance. Let the motion pull her sensitive flesh. Teased her open, thrilling her even without touching her. Until finally, finally, he curled a finger and slid it inside.

"Yes, Simon..."

Two fingers. Still not enough. She writhed on his hand as her vision blurred.

"More..."

"Jess..."

No one could say her name the way he did. No one could make her heart soar like this man.

She moved faster. "Yes..."

Three fingers.

"More!"

He circled. Plunged deeper. Dragged in and out.

She was close, so close to shattering. Wanted to, so badly. But it wasn't enough. Nothing would be enough until she had the real thing.

"Simon, please..." She groped at his jeans. "I need this. I mean... I mean..."

His lips quirked, and his eyes gleamed. Her bear was hungry for more, too.

"I need this, too." His voice went husky as he guided her hand to his crotch. "I need you."

She cupped the front of his jeans. Rubbed up and down. Got on her knees a second later to use both hands on the stubborn zipper.

"Jesus," she muttered. "I might have to go after this with my teeth."

Lust flickered in his eyes. "I wouldn't mind."

She grinned at him and flashed a toothy smile, letting her canines extend just a tiny bit. "Wolf teeth?"

"Maybe not," he joked. Then he caught a breath, and she froze, reading his thoughts.

A bite. *Her* bite. The mating bite. They'd come close a couple of times, way back when. They'd barely held their beasts back from it at times. She flicked her tongue over her lips and watched the pulse beat in his neck. Right there. Right there...

His thumb caressed the hollow of her neck, and she knew he was thinking the same thing. *Right here...*

Mated shifters called the exchange of mating bites the greatest high of their lives, and she could picture it so well. Instinct told her just how it would work. She'd sink her teeth in and carefully, slowly penetrate. Hold on tight and taste him, then keep her tongue over the wound until it closed. She'd do all that while he was buried inside her at the height of sex, and then they'd crash-land into a new life as a mated pair. She'd never be lost or lonely again.

So close... the moonlight seemed to whisper as it flowed into the room.

So close... Simon's mouth cracked open as he focused on her neck.

So easy... Her wolf nodded along.

She leaned closer, and Simon held his breath. Leaving it up to her. The high of her life, there for the taking...

Every atom in her body wanted it. Begged for it. But her mind...

"Too soon," she whispered, shaking herself out of the moonspell.

Simon's nostrils flicked wide, and then he shook his head, too. "Too soon," he agreed.

The last time they'd come this close, they'd decided to wait for exactly the right time.

"Not yet," she whispered, drawing a grin from him. "Not yet."

"But this..." she said, flicking an eyebrow up and reaching for his jeans. "This is not going to wait."

He laughed and watched as she worked the button open and the zipper down. He watched as she slipped a hand inside to touch him, then let his eyes slide shut.

"Perfect," he murmured.

Perfect, just like she remembered. The thick, heated feel of him in her hand. The tingle in the air as both of them became more and more aroused. The need, throbbing deep inside.

It took ages to get the jeans off him, but what did she expect of undressing a bear? His thighs bulged with muscle, and his rear was hard and round. When he sat up to help her, a boxy line of muscle stood up along the length of his abdomen. But when she finally got him out of those jeans... Heaven. Finally, she had her mate again, skin to skin.

She stroked the length of him, guiding him closer as they both rolled. His weight pressed her into the mattress, and their eyes locked.

Love you. Need you. Want you. She sent the sentiment straight into his mind.

He nudged her legs wider. *Love you.* Nestled the head of his cock against her entrance. *Need you.* Pulled her arms up over her head. *Want you.*

She'd barely nodded before he plunged in.

"Yes!" she cried at the searing inner pain.

"Watch me," Simon whispered. "Keep your eyes open. Look at me."

She hadn't even noticed closing them, being so intent on the sweet slide inside. The feel of him stretching her, filling her.

"Yes. . . " she mumbled breathlessly.

When he drew out, it was sweet torture. Then he pushed back in, and that was even better. Her whole body screamed with satisfaction at the feel of him right where he belonged.

"Perfect," he rasped.

"Simon. . . " She pulled her legs higher and tightened her fingers around his.

He rolled his hips and nestled deeper, then pulled back and hammered in again. Then he settled into a rhythm of one slow slide followed by a hard push that she matched with tiny bucks and cries. She kept his hands captive and squeezed him inside until he was groaning with her. The shadows in the room danced faster, too, and a vein stood out on his brow. His biceps bulged, keeping him balanced over her with just the right pressure. Just the right everything.

"Simon," she pleaded, tightening her legs. Pumping him as hard as he pumped into her, panting his name.

"God, Jess. . . " he groaned through gritted teeth, driving her right to the edge. His next thrust was so hard, so fast, she slid up the bed.

Her blood rushed through her veins. Her teeth bit into her lip, but that was only part of the pleasure-pain. Her mouth opened in the silent cry. Every nerve in her body wound tighter and tighter, spiraling out of control. Simon was moving so fast, filling her so deep. . .

"Yes. . . " she moaned as the rush overtook her. "Yes. . . "

Simon panted beside her ear, still going. His balls slapped against her skin. Then he went stiff all over and groaned so deeply, it was more vibration than sound.

"Jess..." The softest, most longing sound she'd ever heard from a bear.

He collapsed over her, and she wrapped her arms and legs around him, keeping him close.

Keeping him forever, her wolf hummed, rolling in drowsy bliss.

He wiped them both off with a shirt, rolled behind her, and spooned her close. Stroked a thumb over her hand, and she stroked back. Saying nothing, feeling everything. Falling gently, peacefully into the sweet silence of sleep.

Chapter Fourteen

"You're serious." Soren looked him square in the eye.

Simon stared right back. Yes, he was serious. Dead serious.

"She's my mate."

Soren gave him a stern look and took another sip of his coffee. Bland coffee Simon had already given up on sipping because it was nowhere near as good as the coffee Jess made. But that's what he got for dragging his brother halfway across town to a corner diner on a Sunday afternoon.

A Sunday afternoon that followed the best sleep of his life. He'd managed to get Jess to sleep in, too, and even if what they'd been up to wasn't only sleep, he'd never felt as rested or as good in his life.

Yep, the best sleep of his life and the best muffin a bear ever did eat. A blueberry oatmeal muffin that burst with juice and sweetness and love. Jess had slipped out of bed an hour before him — obviously, he'd have to work on her definition of sleeping in — and baked a fresh batch, just for him.

It had pretty much been the best morning ever, stretching long past noon. The saloon didn't open until late on Sundays, so there was no rush. Plenty of time to touch, to kiss, and finally, to eat breakfast. It was bliss until Soren stomped downstairs, muttering something about coffee.

Jess had walked by him with a friendly, "Good morning."

"Morning," Soren mumbled back.

Jessica's scent had trailed half a step behind her, thick with the heavy musk of bear. Of satisfaction. Of sex.

Soren's head whipped around. To Jess then back to Simon, then to Jess again. Soren's eyes grew wide, and he batted Simon in the chest.

You telling me that you and she. . . Soren blurted into his mind. Another accusation. *You. . . you. . .*

The fire in his eyes made it clear Soren knew exactly what verb followed the *You.*

Which was what had brought him and Soren to the diner, because the conversation they had to have might stand a better chance of avoiding an all-out fight in a place like this. The two of them were squeezed into a booth way in the corner of the diner, glaring at each other over the Formica table, grateful for the boisterous softball team seated at the opposite side of the establishment, providing enough noise to cover their conversation.

"How could I not be serious about Jess?" Simon said.

"I mean more than serious. I mean sure," Soren snapped.

"Sure, I'm sure. You got a problem with that?" He leaned forward and showed his teeth. His regular human teeth, but his bear fangs weren't far from extending, judging from the pressure on his gums.

Soren bristled, unimpressed. Really bristled with considerably more hair showing on his arms and neck than normally would. Both of them were a breath away from shifting, itching to fight.

114

Simon didn't blink. If he had to fight his brother into accepting the truth, he would. Never mind that his older brother beat him every time they'd fought, either as kids or men. He'd take Soren on. He'd do what he had to. He'd do *anything* he had to do.

Like flexing his fingers against the table, fighting to keep his claws sheathed. Why the hell was Soren so bitter about the idea?

Somewhere across the diner, a woman laughed, and they both looked up. An older woman patted the shoulder of the man next to her in an easy, practiced motion she'd probably repeated over the past twenty or thirty years.

They both watched for a second, and when Soren turned back, Simon saw him in a new light.

Maybe Soren wasn't so much mad as sad. Still in mourning, as he always would be, for his lost mate.

Simon sucked in a long, dry breath and started again, in a whisper this time.

"Look, if it were Sarah..."

Soren's head snapped up, his eyes fierce.

Simon plowed on. "If it were Sarah, wouldn't you risk anything to get her back?"

The fire in Soren's eyes burned brighter, then slowly died out. He dipped his chin so far, it nearly touched his chest. "I'd die for her." Then he winced and closed his eyes. He didn't say the rest, but it was written all over his face. *But I didn't. I failed.*

A painfully quiet minute passed in which Simon relived the soul-sucking despair of the past six months. Yeah, he knew exactly how Soren felt. And it hurt almost as much to be the lucky one. The one with a second chance.

115

"Look," Simon said, as softly as he could. "I know you'd do anything for her. I'd do anything to help you get her. But..."

Soren stared at the table. They both knew the *but* was an obstacle that no amount of wishing, dreaming, or fighting would overcome. Soren shook his head and downed the last of his coffee with an expression so blank, it hurt Simon more than the angry version did. Soren was hiding the pain. Denying it, just as he had these past dreary months.

"No," Soren said in a raspy voice. When he looked up again, the bear had drifted out of his eyes, replaced by a weary resignation. "I guess I don't have a problem with that."

Simon exhaled slowly, but his brother wasn't done.

Soren leaned closer and finished his thought. "But the Twin Moon wolves might."

Simon threw his head back. Christ, what would it take to win his mate?

"Why would they?" Simon didn't know everyone on Twin Moon Ranch, but he knew there were a couple of non-wolves mixed in. A handful of humans, a wild boar...

"Think about it. They've got their own to protect. They don't want Blue Bloods sniffing around here any more than we do. And really, what do the wolves of Twin Moon Ranch owe us?"

Simon groped for words. Soren was right. The wolves didn't really owe them anything. They didn't owe Jess and Janna, either. They had been willing to help out, but how much longer would they be willing to help if the newcomers drew rogues into their corner of the world?

Not long, Soren's sharp gaze said. *Not long.*

116

"Maybe Tina could..." Simon started.

Soren cut him off with a sharp shake of the head. "Are you really going to ask her to go that far out on a limb for us?"

Tina was kind and generous and principled to the core. She'd help smooth things over with the wolf pack if they asked. But she was also mated to a man who'd been human before she turned him wolf. Tina was building an addition on her house that could only mean the two of them were hoping for kids.

Now Simon was the one shaking his head. No, he couldn't ask any more of Tina. Couldn't put her at risk, too.

"Us being bears, Jess being a wolf..." Soren went on. "The Blue Bloods would come looking..."

Soren didn't have to spell it out.

Simon pulled a sugar packet closer and ripped it to shreds, just to have something to destroy. His bear had already been picturing the apartment over the saloon as home. As the start of a new den, maybe even a real clan someday. He and Jess could take a room at the far end of the house, and Soren and Janna could...

He caught himself there. Did he really expect Soren and Janna to be daily witnesses to his newfound bliss? Well, Janna, maybe. She wouldn't mind, and a woman like her was bound to find a mate of her own someday. But Soren...

He glanced at his brother. Damn.

He could play the surly uncle, his bear suggested.

Damn bear had everything figured out, did he? Although cubs just might soften Soren up...

Simon pushed the thought out of his mind and tried pulling some kind of plan together.

The bell over the diner door jingled merrily, but the man stomping in under it looked more like a thundercloud than the sunshine outside. Simon cursed under his breath. What he needed — fast — was a plan that would convince the Twin Moon alpha that he and Soren could maintain peace among wolves. Good wolves and bad wolves.

He had to work hard to remember the *good wolves* part, watching Ty Hawthorne stomp up. A very unhappy alpha on a mission to bruise, maim, and possibly kill, judging by the smoldering look on his face. A dark cloud of disapproval traveled ahead of him, practically flattening everything in sight.

He smacked a newspaper on the table, and the people three booths over jumped. "What the hell were you thinking?"

Simon blinked. "Um... "

Soren turned the paper to read it and swore under his breath.

What? Simon shot the question into his brother's mind. *What?*

Soren's arm blocked the newspaper, but when he turned it, Simon saw the photo on the lower right.

"Shit."

Lost girl saved from inferno! the headline blazed. *Five thousand acres burn. Local heroine...*

Shit, shit, shit. Even the wave of pride that hit him didn't stop his gut from churning. There was Jess, front and center, in a paper all of northern Arizona read.

It was one of those prize-winning photographs that managed to capture all of the energy, the drama, the relief of last night. Jess stood on one side, smudged with soot, leaning over the little girl and her teary mother with a bolstering smile. The kind of newspaper article he'd frame and hang in the saloon, if it weren't for one thing.

"If anyone sees this and recognizes her..." Ty trailed off.

Soren's phone lay on the table, and it peeped with an incoming text, but no one paid it any mind. Not at a time like this.

Simon snatched the paper up and started skim-reading. There was no mention of Jessica's name, nor his. But the photo had captured Jess perfectly. It was only a question of time before she was recognized. He could see it now. Some asshole from Mike's Hardware would see the paper, recognize Jess, and call out the press.

His heart beat faster. And with the rogues after Jess...

"Shit."

"Shit is right," Ty barked, barely under his breath. "Where is she now?"

He wasn't that stupid. Kyle, the wolf-cop, was parked innocuously across from the saloon, keeping an eye on things while the bears were away.

"Kyle's there."

Ty gritted his teeth, still not satisfied. He thumped a fist on the newspaper. "What the hell were you think-ing?"

The couple in the neighboring booth tossed a couple of bills on their table and fled.

"I was thinking, get the kid out of the fire," Simon blurted. "Get my mate out of the fire."

Ty froze, and Soren winced.

"Your mate?" the wolf growled, low and menacing.

It was all he could do not to growl back. Jess wasn't Ty Hawthorne's to growl over. She was his! She was his bear's! She was...

He let his eyes slide shut. She was her own damn person, and if he couldn't manage more than caveman tactics, she'd never accept him as her mate.

Soren's phone peeped again, and Simon barely held back from flattening it with his fist.

"My mate," he declared, looking up into the alpha's dark eyes.

The wolf's glare pulsed with power, with demand. But way in the back, something else flickered gently, like a single candle in the eye of the storm. Understanding, maybe. Ty Hawthorne had a mate of his own. He would respect the mating bond, right?

The glare went on and on, and just when Simon thought he'd died of suffocation, the wolf let up.

Understanding glowed yellow under the black. Understanding and respect. Not that the alpha would let them off easy.

"The last thing we need is to draw the Blue Bloods' attention here," Ty said, still looming over the table.

"We hunted them once," Soren said, butting in to relieve him. "We can do it again."

But that was the thing, and all three of them knew it. Simon and Soren had already hunted the murderers down. Each and every one involved in the Black River massacre. But where one fell, two more sprung up, united by a sick ideology of hate.

Ty shook his head, and Simon waited for the alpha to blurt out a reply. One that said something like, *Get the hell out of our territory. Good-bye and good luck.*

Where would he and Jess go? What would they do?

"No," Ty said. "We need to think this over."

We? Simon's ears perked up.

"Rally our allies..." the wolf went on. "Gather intel..."

Simon studied the alpha. Was Ty saying what his bear hoped for?

"We're working on it," Ty said. "Believe me, we're working on it. But we need time."

"And in the meantime..." Simon held his breath.

Ty kept up the glare, but the force of it was focused elsewhere now. On the real enemy — the Blue Blood rogues. "In the meantime, we need to bring those two she-wolves to the ranch. To protect them."

Simon just about jumped to his feet to protest, but Soren's phone beeped again. All three of them turned their anger to the device.

"Get it," Ty barked.

Simon looked out the diner windows, clenching his fists. He should be the one protecting Jess, not the wolves.

"Damn," Soren cursed, looking at the text. "Kyle's been called to an accident. He's had to leave the saloon."

Simon would have whipped around to check the message with his own eyes, but a red pickup driving past grabbed his attention. A big Ford with tinted windows and Oklahoma plates.

"We need to get back there soon," Soren said.

Simon gripped the edge of the table, still intent on the road outside. Why did that pickup alarm his bear so?

A second truck drove past, almost a carbon copy of the first, and he tracked it with his eyes. The diner door opened with a departing customer, and the scent of the street wafted in. Tarmac, heating under the sun. A streak of oil, spilled on the road. And a distant hint of a warm-blooded creature with ice in its soul.

Simon jumped out of the booth. "Rogues! We need to get there right now!"

"Rogues," Ty hissed, nearly in the same breath.

The three of them sprinted for the door, ignoring the waitress' squeak of protest.

"My truck!" Soren shouted. "Get in my truck!"

Ty's vehicle was too far, so all three of them piled in. Soren revved the engine to life and peeled onto the street, leaving tire marks and the scent of burning rubber.

A horn blared. Ty pointed at the red vehicles, speeding through an intersection ahead.

"Go! Go!" Simon yelled.

Ty punched the keys of his phone, muttering Kyle's name.

The light turned yellow, and Soren stomped on the gas.

The light turned red. Soren swore and leaned over the steering wheel, racing on.

Something roared from the right. Screamed, like a meteor hurtling through space. Simon turned just in time to see the grill of a massive eighteen-wheeler barrel down on the side window.

"Shit!"

The next thing he knew, Soren's truck was skidding sideways. Metal groaned. Fiberglass crunched. His bones cried out. Then everything went black, and his world turned off like a light.

Chapter Fifteen

Jess hummed while she cleaned the bar counter. She and Janna had everything ready to go for the evening rush, which probably wouldn't be much of a rush, given the fact that the rodeo was still running on the outskirts of town. That was where all the action was that evening, which suited her just fine. She was still processing it all. A night of near-terror that had turned into peace. The feeling of two joined souls instead of a single, lonely one.

She'd slept the soundest, deepest sleep she had in years and awoken to Simon stroking her face with wonder in his eyes. *Are you really here? Are you really mine?*

She wanted to ask him the same thing.

Still wanted to ask him, but he'd gone off with Soren. Never mind. It gave her a chance to replay the morning and cherish every detail once more. Like when she kissed him in the wee hours of morning, then grimaced.

"That bad, huh?" he had asked.

"No!" she'd said a little too loudly for dawn on a Sunday, and then again, more quietly. "No. It's just this...this..." She held up a finger blackened with soot.

"Grime," he filled in, kissing it right off her skin.

The kissing part, she liked. But the grime threatened to bring her old nightmares back. So they'd slowly rolled out of bed and headed toward the bathroom for a shower.

She had padded out of her room a step ahead of Simon, then whispered back to him. "Coming?"

She turned to glance back and froze at the sight of Simon rubbing up against the doorjamb to her room. Rubbing good and hard, marking his turf. The way he'd nuzzled her in bed, marking her as his, too.

And the crazy thing was, she didn't even mind. Didn't mind the tight squeeze into the claw-foot bathtub, either, even if it wasn't designed to shower two.

"I'll do you, you do me," he had half whispered, half growled.

And yeah, he did her all right. Did her good and well once they'd dried off and headed out — to his room, this time. He couldn't get her to the bed fast enough for either of their tastes, but when he had...

She'd hummed in satisfaction afterward and snuggled against him, just like before. Feeling so clean. So fresh. So blissfully worn out that the next time she'd opened her eyes, it was light. Bright daylight, shining into Simon's room. A room just as sparsely furnished as Soren's, except for one thing. There was a photo pinned to the wall above the bed. A wallet-size photo worn around the edges. It showed a lush green background and two familiar faces that made her catch her breath.

A photo of the two of them they'd snapped one perfect Montana afternoon at the edge of a carnival that had come through the county. Simon stood behind her, half a head taller and nearly twice as wide, ducking his chin to rest on her shoulder. She was wearing his flannel shirt and sporting her old hairstyle. Both of them so young and in love and clueless about what would come next.

"You kept this picture..." She traced the edge, barely breathing.

He nodded slowly. "Took it with me when I went back East."

Her eyes had filled with warm tears, looking at her past. "Janna and I lost everything the night the Blue Bloods came. Everything. Every person, every thing. Our families. Our home. Albums, keepsakes..." She fingered the photo gingerly and gulped the tears back.

He didn't say anything. Just pulled her into his arms and held her tight, telling her she hadn't quite lost everything. She still had him. Her faithful bear, who'd never stopped loving her, after all.

Just as she'd never stopped loving him. She'd tried and tried to hate him, but it never really worked. For good reason.

Destiny.

She'd lain quietly pondering that for the next few minutes. Was still pondering now, hours later. Being with Simon felt so right. More right than the past three years without him, that was for sure.

"A hell of a night," he had whispered with a wry grin.

She'd just nodded. A hell of a night.

But life went on. The clock kept ticking, right up to opening time, and right up to the time when Soren had hauled Simon away on some errand, promising they'd be right back.

Which meant it was just her and Janna, getting the saloon ready for opening time. Jess wiped glasses behind the bar while Janna prepped the silverware, grumbling the whole time. Her sister had been uncharacteristically grumpy ever since she'd tumbled out of bed at noon.

"You okay?" she tried.

"Fine," Janna barked back.

Hungover, maybe? Jess didn't ask. All she knew was that her sister smelled faintly of cigarette smoke and stale sweat, even after a shower. Bar smells, in other words, which was typical for Janna on a Saturday night. The grumpy mood wasn't, though, and neither was the scent layered over the rest. The faint scent of cowboy. Leather, oak, a touch of horse, and a tiny trace of sweat. The nice kind of sweat, with a whole lot of man in it.

The next time Janna walked by, Jess took a second surreptitious sniff, and her eyebrows promptly shot up. It wasn't wolf-cowboy scent. It was pure human. Cole-scent, to be precise. Had Janna been dancing with the broken cowboy last night? His scent was clear enough to hint that they'd been slow dancing, and close. What else had she done with Cole last night?

But Janna wouldn't say a word, and Jess didn't pry.

The saloon doors opened with one creak, then another, and booted feet clomped into the saloon. Jess didn't turn or glance in the bar mirror. She need one more second of daydreaming about Simon and fate and maybe even forever, and then she'd be back on the job.

"Be right there," Janna said, forcing a perky voice. She turned from the corner table to the newcomers. "What can I get y—"

Jess spun around at the alarm in her sister's voice.

"You," the man nearest the bar said simply. "We want you."

Jess stared at him. A middle-aged man clad in blinding white-on-white with a face that gave nothing away. Two younger, burlier men flanked him, and another filed in behind, letting the doors swing in weighty silence.

Jess didn't need to have ever laid eyes on the men to know who they were. Didn't need her nose to finally register the stale rogue smell. These were wolves. Rogues. Blue Bloods, as the blue rings tattooed on their fingers proclaimed.

Purity! Purity! The eerie chant rose up from her memories.

"Now, we figured a couple of young and impressionable she-wolves might make the mistake of associating with the wrong species..." the man in white started, speaking casually. Like a minister warming up to the body of a sermon that would build to fire and brimstone before too long.

Whyte. Victor Whyte. The leader of the purist rogues.

Jess looked around wildly for some weapon or means of escape.

"The wrong kind?" Janna sneered. "You mean, as opposed to you?"

Victor Whyte smiled indulgently and went on as if he hadn't heard.

"But to make the mistake of associating with bears a second time, why, that sounds like those she-wolves haven't learned their lesson." He flashed his teeth — long, wolf teeth. When Whyte leaned in a moment later, his tone dropped to pure malice. "We're here to teach them."

Janna brandished her beverage tray like a weapon. "Sure," she spat back. "Teach me."

Jess inched backward, trying to think. Four-to-two were bad odds, whether they shifted to wolf form or stayed on two feet. The front door was blocked by one of the rogues — a big one. Too big to get past. The antique Winchester hanging high over the bar wasn't loaded, and even if she got it down before the rogues got to her, she'd never make it to the silver bullets Soren kept in the cash register in time.

The preacher-type sighed and looked at the burly man to his left. "What do you think, Brett?"

Back door, Jess yelled to Janna in her thoughts. *We make a run for it.*

Janna threw her a stubborn look.

Four of them against two of us, Janna. Come on!

The rogue named Brett showed a row of crooked, stained teeth. "I think they want to learn." The men's banter was breezy, like a couple of Midwesterners chatting about baseball or their crops. "Need to learn."

"Need to be taught their lesson," a third grumbled from over by the door. A younger one, itching for a fight. Or worse than a fight, judging by the way his eyes traced Janna's form-fitting shirt.

Janna shot him a disdainful look but started inching toward the back doorway.

"Yes," Whyte sighed. "I think you're right. Such a pity these nice girls have to learn the hard way."

At his nod, the one called Brett stepped forward, moving from shadow to light and into shadow again. For an instant, Jess saw the innocent teen he might once have been. Had he been a runaway from a pack ruled by a harsh alpha? Perhaps a young wolf who'd supported a power play and ended up on the losing side, then been cast out of his home pack? Either way, he was young, bitter, and easily molded to a cause. Any cause, as long as it came with acceptance and the illusion of power.

Janna kept her tray high and backed toward Jess, who eyed the space around her. Maybe if she used a chair...

"Now, we can do this the hard way, or we can do this the easy way."

Whyte made it sound so reasonable. But *easy*, Jess figured, was these rogues taking her and Janna off someplace to beat and murder in cold blood.

"Maybe we can play a little first," the one by the door added in a husky voice.

Make that beat, rape, and then murder.

"Of course," Whyte told him, waving a dismissive hand. "You'll get your chance. Each of you. If you can stand the thought of a wolf who's whored herself to a bear." His gaze turned to Jess, oozing disgust.

She snarled out loud, barely keeping her wolf in check. "Says the man who's whored himself to a sick cause. Says the murderer."

His gaze grew dark. "Educator. Savior. Protector of pure shifter blood."

Pure. She could have snorted. Pure was her bond to Simon that had held up for so long.

The big one nodded gravely and started gushing the gospel he'd obviously heard over and over again. "So few shifters left on earth. The ancient bloodlines must be upheld."

"Bloodlines," Jess said slowly, trying to buy Janna time to inch closer to the hallway leading to the back. "Sure." He made it sound like shifters were royalty, when they were the last scrappy survivors of what had once been a widespread breed.

"Ever heard of inbreeding, idiot?" Janna threw in.

"We cannot let the bloodlines weaken." He looked surprised when Jess didn't agree. "We must protect our purity."

"Pure bullshit, if you ask me," Janna muttered, closer to the hallway. Jess counted her every step, holding her breath. Soon Janna would be close enough to make a run for it, and Jess would follow right behind. "Protect your own purity all you want. Just don't go messing with mine."

"Says the woman who reeks of..." The rogue sniffed in her direction then cocked a haughty eyebrow. "Human?"

Jess stuck her jaw out and glared. "Go protect your so-called purity somewhere else. No one wants you here."

"Oh, but we want to be here. Just not for long." The leader cast a glance out the front windows. That was one thing on the sisters' side. It was broad daylight. Even a crazed rogue wouldn't shift into wolf form in public, and he was just as unlikely to murder her here.

Mike from the hardware store walked past the front windows and tipped his hat. "Hello, ladies!"

Jess and Janna exchanged desperate glances. Did they dare call for help?

The rogue nearest the door growled under his breath. *Do it. Call him. I'll kill him right before I kill you.*

Jess waved weakly to Mike and watched as he sauntered out of sight. Shifters had extraordinary strength; Mike would have to be a prizefighter to stand a chance against the rogues. She couldn't get him involved.

Janna shot her a look. *A bear would come in handy right around now.*

God, where were the Voss brothers?

Chapter Sixteen

"If you'll just step this way..." Victor Whyte motioned toward the front door and spoke in a sticky-sweet voice.

Jess took a deep breath. Much as she'd like the bear brothers to show up now, she hadn't spent the last few years waiting to be rescued like a damsel in distress. She wouldn't start now.

On three, we run for the back. Ready? she called into her sister's mind. The rogues couldn't hear her thoughts the way her sister could, and thank God for that.

She put up her hands and did her best to look meek. "Okay, okay, we don't want any trouble. Just leave our friends alone."

"Don't worry," the rogue clad in white said. "We won't hurt a fly."

A lie, and she knew it, but she could pretend.

"Don't worry, we'll show you ladies a good time," the one by the door grinned, staring at Jessica's chest.

Right. A good time.

One, she called to Janna.

Her sister gave a tiny nod.

Two...

She edged out from behind the bar.

Three!

Jess grabbed for the nearest stool and hurled it at exactly the same moment that Janna frisbeed her tray into Whyte's throat. Two surprised cries went out, and he staggered. Not for long but enough to give them a chance.

They dashed down the hallway, into the dimmer back room, and raced for the rear door. It flew open in front of them, and they both screeched to a halt. An even bigger rogue stepped through the door, grinning ear to ear.

"Going somewhere, ladies?"

"Shit," Janna yelped, backing away.

Jess grabbed Janna and pulled her to the small bar in the back room just as the other rogues ran in from the front. She swiveled her head left, then right. Trapped.

"Damn it," Janna muttered. She grabbed a broom and brandished it like a lance.

Jess took up a barstool and held it up in defense. "Get out of my saloon! Now!"

Technically, it wasn't her saloon, but it sure felt like it. Her new home. Her future. She wasn't about to give it up without a fight.

"Get them!" Whyte hissed to his men.

We can do this, Janna said, sounding shaky as the others closed in.

Jess nodded. *We have to do this.*

"If only those idiots had killed you along with the rest," Whyte snarled. "Those who dare soil shifter bloodlines shall all feel our wrath."

The other three closed in, and Janna stabbed the broomstick at the nearest rogue's chest. He fell back with a grunt. "How's that for feeling wrath, asshole?"

Jess, meanwhile, swung the barstool at the rogue advancing toward her.

"Purity. Purity..." Whyte started chanting in an eerie monotone.

A third rogue muscled his way in, and Jess snarled. Her heart pounded, and her vision went red. The night the Blue Bloods killed her family, she hadn't had the chance to fight back, but she did now. And she'd use it, damn it.

The nearest rogue raised a hand to punch, and she batted it away with the stool. Once. Twice. And the third time, he caught the stool and wrenched it out of her hands.

"Now what, she-wolf?" he grinned.

She grabbed a whiskey bottle off the bar, smashed the end, and held up the jagged neck. "Try me. Just try..."

The smile vanished from his face as he pulled back.

"Idiot! Get them!" Whyte cried, though he shied away from the action himself. Which made it more like four rogues against two she-wolves rather than five on two. Odds she liked better, even if they were still slim.

Then another rogue hurried through the front door and she cursed again.

The two rogues they'd caught off guard had picked themselves up again, and all five advanced.

"You had your chance to come peacefully," the leader scolded as his men moved in.

Jess clutched the bottle neck tightly and swung it in an arc. *Okay, we'll shift and fight our way out,* she called to Janna. *Ready?* Speed was their best weapon — a swift shift and then escape. She had no clue if they could pull it off, but it seemed like their best chance.

You bet I'm ready. These assholes stole our past, Janna grunted into her mind by way of a pep talk. *We'll show them how Black River wolves can fight.*

A fight to the death, and they both knew it.

Jess gritted her teeth. *These assholes want our future, too.* She'd fight with the strength of two wolves, just on the basis of that.

A shout sounded from the front room, followed by a crash, and everyone's head turned.

Janna flashed a triumphant grin. *Yes! They're finally here!*

By *they*, Janna surely meant the bears, but the man who came hurtling down the hallway a second later wasn't Simon or Soren or even Kyle, the cop who'd stopped by earlier.

"Cole?" Janna blurted, incredulous as the cowboy strode into sight, looking taller and more menacing than Jess had ever seen him. "Oh God, Cole!" Janna's cry was a mixture of relief and terror, because even a rough-and-tumble cowboy like Cole wouldn't stand a chance against the rogues.

"Janna," he said in a growly voice. He eyed the strangers with dark, dangerous eyes. "Uninvited company?"

For a second, everyone froze. Then Cole clenched his fists and advanced on the nearest intruders. Angry. Livid. Positively lethal.

"No, Cole..." Jess cried. The last thing they needed was to draw a human into a shifter fight.

Too late. The rogues snarled but stayed in human form, and a split second later, chaos broke out.

A rogue swung a fist, but Cole ducked, moving with uncanny speed and pure athletic grace. He straightened with an uppercut that threw the rogue back. Jess hurled a bottle at the rogue beside him. Janna swung the broom, using the distraction to catch another rogue off guard.

"Get them!" Whyte shouted, skittering to one side.

"Cole!" Janna yelled, slamming the broom into the nearest rogue's groin.

Jess grabbed another bottle and went for the closest enemy. "Janna, watch out!"

Janna spun just in time to ward off the man going for her back, sending him Jessica's way. She sliced his cheek open with the bottle and snarled.

She and Janna kicked. They hurled chairs and insults. They fought dirty, desperately. With stools, bottles, and even a dustpan. And surprisingly, she, Janna, and Cole held the rogues for a minute or two.

Then another two Blue Bloods ran in from the front, and the tide turned.

"Oh!" Janna crashed to the floor when a rogue took her feet out with a kick.

"Get up!" Jess yelled, flinging her bottle at the rogue who grabbed her sister's hair. When she reached for another bottle, a big, thick hand clamped over her arm and twisted it, hard.

Cole sent one rogue flying, but the new newcomers got him from behind and threw him across the room.

"Cole!" Janna screamed as he smashed against the wall and crumpled to the floor.

Whyte cackled. "Purity. Purity..."

Jess spun and kneed her attacker in the groin while Janna butted her way free. But a moment later, the others charged in in overwhelming numbers. Jess clawed at the hands reaching, pulling, yanking at her, but it was a losing battle, and she knew it. Janna's shouts grew more harried, too. More like prayers than battle cries.

Christ, they'd need a miracle to get out of this now.

The rogues fought with renewed vigor. They'd underestimated the she-wolves at first, but not any more. Which made their kicks harder, their punches more powerful.

"Cole!" Janna yelped as the biggest rogue grabbed her by the throat.

But Cole lay motionless where he'd fallen. Jess ducked too late to avoid another punch, and suddenly, all she could see were stars.

"Finally," the leader rogue hissed in the eerie silence that ensued. "Kill that one, then that one, then her."

Jess didn't know who was *one* or *her*, but it was all the same in the end. She had to get up!

But she couldn't, because a booted foot pushed down on the back of her neck. Just a little pressure, and he'd snap it. And that kind of injury, even a quick-healing shifter couldn't beat. She was strong, but not immortal.

"No! No!" Janna kicked and cried, but she was fading fast.

Get up! Fight! Survive! Every nerve in Jessica's body screamed for her to try something — anything! — but she was powerless. Even shifting into wolf form wouldn't help her get free.

It was the end. God, just when she'd discovered a new reason for living, her life would be ripped away.

"I told you," the leader tut-tutted. "The hard way, or the easy way."

She closed her eyes, but they shot open a second later when a familiar voice growled from the hallway. "Hard way, asshole."

Simon?

A furious roar shook the room. Part human, part bear.

The room exploded into shouts. Grunts. Growls. The crushing weight lifted from her neck and flew away. Boots flashed by as she lay on the floor, gasping for breath.

Get up. Get up...

The feet in her field of vision scrambled this way and that, most of them heading for the back door. Jess rolled toward the bar and hauled herself up. Her arms shook. Her knees wobbled. Her breath came in desperate pants. The only sense she could rely on was smell, telling her Simon was back at last. Simon, looking strangely ragged, like he'd come right from some other fight. Looking positively furious and bent on revenge.

She saw him blur past and send the biggest rogue flying out a window with an ear-splitting crash.

A second shape rushed by. Soren, bent at the waist like a battering ram. He slammed into the nearest rogue and hurled him bodily out the open door.

Jess swayed on her feet, clutching the bar.

Behind her, a rogue screamed in agony, and a bone snapped.

"Get. Out. Of. My. Saloon," Simon roared, barely human.

Soren hauled another rogue off Janna by the scruff of his neck and squeezed until the man turned red, then threw him against the wall like a rag doll.

"Cole! Cole!" Janna crawled toward the fallen cowboy.

A fierce wolf snarl came from the hallway, and Jess spotted the Twin Moon alpha, Ty Hawthorne. There wasn't much for him to do by then but glare, but it was enough. Any rogue left standing ran out the door, fleeing for his life. Including Victor Whyte, who paused just long enough on the threshold to shake his fist. "We'll be back," he shouted, then ran. Jess shuddered as he yelled it again and again.

"We'll be back..."

Soren gave brief chase, then stood looming at the door, daring the enemy to try again.

One last rogue got to his feet and headed for Simon with hate in his eyes. "Impure. You are impure."

Jessica's vision was still a bit shaky; all she saw was a blur. Human Simon, with huge bear claws, swiping at the man's chest. A splash of blood, a choked cry. A dull thump.

"Cole..." Janna cried, somewhere to her right.

Jess swayed a second later, and just when she was sure she'd crumple, two thick arms circled her waist.

"Got you," Simon whispered, clutching her in his arms. "Got you."

She wrapped her arms around him, closed her eyes, and whispered back. "Got you, too."

An injured wolf limped toward the shattered window to make his escape. Simon's head popped up, but Jess tugged him back. "Let him go."

"He'll be back, Jess."

She shrugged. "Let them try to keep a she-wolf from her mate."

Simon's eyes went wide. "Mate? You mean it?"

She kissed him, then buried her face in his neck, sniffing deeply. "Mine." She nodded. "Mate."

Epilogue

Two weeks later...

The first beams of sunrise warmed Jessica's cheek, and she turned away, snuggling closer to her mate.

Simon snored lightly in some happy dream, but his arm tightened around her in automatic response. She smiled and stroked his arm. Night or day, awake or asleep, he seemed to know just where she was and just what she needed. It had been that way ever since they'd exchanged mating bites in one thrilling, passionate night not long after the fight.

Not that they strayed far from each other's sides these days, but still. Jess had the feeling Simon could pinpoint her anywhere on the continent, just as she could him.

She watched him sleep, fascinated by a shifter that big, that ferocious, turned so gentle and calm. Serene, like the feeling that washed over her just from looking at him.

God, how had she ever lived without her bear?

She traced his eyebrow, barely touching. The pain of the past wasn't gone, but it was buried under layers of joy as thick as her grandmother's quilts. She could stay snuggled there all day.

He took a deeper breath and woke, just like that. Another bear thing. Some days, he'd be bleary-eyed until close to noon. But if she touched him in just the right way... a switch went on in him, and there he'd be, wide awake, catching her hand with his.

"Mmm," he hummed, rubbing his chin along her jaw.

She could have purred out loud. Oops. Wait. She did purr out loud.

Simon laughed, because he could read her every thought these days unless she kept them carefully tucked away. Which she only did on rare occasions. If, for example, a girl wanted to keep secret what kind of muffins she'd slipped out of bed to bake for her bear that morning and how many, then yes, she needed to keep some secrets, too. All for his own good.

"What are you so proud of, my mate?" he asked, sniffing his way along her neck.

Her toes flexed, danced, tingled. God, she loved it when he did that. Any contact around the scar of her mating bite turned her on like a light. A red light with very naughty ideas and just enough time to try them out before the muffins were done.

She rolled on top of him. "Proud of you," she said, kissing his brow.

His inner bear preened just a bit. She could tell from the shine in his eyes.

"Proud of us, too." She slid her lips closer to his mouth, ready to claim it with a sloppy kiss.

Simon slid his hands farther up her torso, igniting every nerve in her body. "Proud of wha—"

She cut him off. They could talk or they could play, and nothing beat waking up to the latter. And nothing beat kissing Simon. She swept her tongue over his lips, and when she opened her mouth, he did, too, letting her in.

Such a soulful, drugging kiss, she nearly whimpered into it. She threaded her fingers into his hair for a better grip and started rocking her hips against his.

You're purring, my mate, he whispered into her mind.

I'm not the only one, she whispered back.

She inhaled the rest of the kiss, and when she came up for air a second later, Simon rolled them both. He came out on top, looking awfully pleased with himself. His biceps bulged, supporting just enough of his weight to prevent crushing her completely while keeping her deliciously pinned.

Hmm. Mine. Mate, he growled, grinding against her.

She wound her legs around his waist and growled back. No need for much foreplay, not in the state she was in.

Mine, he groaned, driving deep in.

She held on tight and took another magic carpet ride, courtesy of her bear. The bear who floated her over clouds, dragged her over hot coals of pleasure, and made her cry his name again and again. She tried not to make too much noise and failed miserably.

Make all the noise you want, my mate. His voice was gritty as he thrust harder, pushing her further and further off the edge.

When he came, it was with enough power, enough passion to make both of them shudder for a full minute before sinking back into the mattress and into each other's arms.

Perfect. Life was perfect. Love didn't get better than this.

"Maybe it does." He grinned and started touching her, getting her wound up all over again.

Her alarm chimed, making him groan as she rolled to the side of the bed. Well, technically, she rolled to the side of the mattress, because they still hadn't gotten around to getting a bed. Probably never would, because the mattress suited their animal natures perfectly. They could roll in, roll out. Slumber in animal form, as they'd done a few times. That was its own special pleasure — turning around the bed three times, then going to sleep spooned within the curve of her mate's massive, furry body.

"Too early to get up," Simon protested, pulling her back into his arms.

"I have to take the muffins out."

His eyes lit up. "Berry muffins?"

She laughed. "Come and find out."

A quick shower later, she padded down the stairs, following the murmur of Soren's deep bass to the front room. It was Sunday morning and the saloon was closed. So who could he be talking to?

She pulled two dozen steaming muffins from the oven, set them on a wire rack, and carried them into the saloon.

"Good morning," she called, seeing Soren with two of the Twin Moon wolves: Ty Hawthorne and his sister, Tina.

Ty's and Soren's heads whipped around. Their noses followed the muffins Jess carried toward their booth.

Tina smiled at Jess and stuck an elbow in her brother's ribs.

"Good morning," Tina said pointedly.

"Morning," Ty hastened to add. His eyes stayed on the muffins, though, just like Soren's, and Jess nearly laughed out loud. If she'd known how easy it was to tame tough alphas with nothing more than an old family recipe, she'd have started baking from day one.

Simon ambled up behind her. "Hey! You giving away my muffins again?"

She held up the rack in her right hand. "These are yours."

He made a little *Hmpf* sound, grabbed the coffeepot, and came over to refill everyone's mugs.

"So, back to business," Soren said a moment later, wiping the crumbs from his mouth.

Ty nodded and leaned in, and suddenly the boys were men again.

"Right. We extend the lease on the saloon by another twelve months," Ty said.

"For starters," Tina added with a wink that said the contract could be extended as long as they wanted. "Twelve months is just the standard around here."

Jess bit her lip, and when Simon squeezed her hand, she squeezed back. They'd been so worried that the wolves of Twin Moon Ranch would send them packing after the rogue attack. After all, it was their fault the Blue Bloods had stepped on Twin Moon turf. Apparently, they'd worried for nothing.

Jessica's soul sang. *We can stay! We can stay!*

Simon grinned at her. Even Soren looked relieved, though he hid it by sipping his coffee.

She looked around the saloon. It had taken ages to clean up, but everyone had pitched in. She leaned against Simon and thought back to the fight. Or rather, the good parts, after the fight.

Like Simon, holding her like he'd never let go.

Like Janna, crying in relief when Cole opened his eyes and blinked.

Like Ty, shaking hands with Soren with a new kind of respect.

Back to the memory of Simon laughing when she'd looked him up and down and said, "Jesus. You look like you got hit by a truck."

The three men — Simon, Soren, and Ty — had looked at each other without uttering a word. When she'd learned they really had been hit by a truck, she'd shrieked.

"Shifters." Simon had shrugged. "We heal fast."

"That fast?" she'd gaped.

He'd just hugged her closer. "When we have reason to."

She looked around, remembering all that, and squeezed his hand again, not quite believing her luck.

Her relief must have shown, because Tina gave her a reassuring smile. "You and the bears strengthen our pack."

Ty swallowed another bite of muffin and nodded in agreement. "Can always use capable allies guarding this edge of our territory."

A win-win, and thank goodness, because Jess loved the saloon almost as much as she loved Simon.

Tina rolled her eyes at Ty's comment and shot Jess a look that said, *By capable, he means he's damn impressed by how you and your bears fight.*

Jess smiled. Technically, only Simon was her bear. But, yes, the brothers were a package deal, so Soren's was hers in a way, too. If only she could find him his own mate...

"Now, about other business," Ty started, looking at Soren.

Other business probably meant a strategy on how to prevent further Blue Blood attacks, Jess figured and immediately tensed up.

Tina slid out of the booth and motioned her toward the front door. "Come. We need to have our own business talk."

Jess followed her reluctantly, and Simon watched her go with a look so mournful, even Tina laughed. "I'm not taking her to the moon! Just next door."

Tina prodded her out the swinging saloon doors and into the bright sunlight. It was midmorning on a Sunday, and the streets were quiet but for the sound of birdsong and the jingle of Tina's keys. She picked one from a ring and opened the door of the neighboring shop.

"Have you ever been in here?" Tina asked.

Jess shook her head and looked around when Tina led her in.

"It used to be a small art gallery. Before that, a café. We haven't been able to find a renter for it in years."

Even with dust and scraps of paper littering the floor, it was a homey, cozy place. Jess looked up and realized her bedroom was directly overhead. Her new bedroom, that is. The one at the far end of the hallway. She and Simon had moved in there so it wouldn't be her room or his room, but *their* room.

"This place has one-third of the building's street frontage," Tina went on, leading her toward the back. "Great location, but we never found anyone with the business sense to run it well. The saloon takes up the other two-thirds. The art gallery only ever used the front room, but back here..."

She swung a creaky door wide, and Jessica's mouth fell open. Stainless steel counters ran around the perimeter of the room, with another creating an island in the middle of the space. The entire back wall was lined with big, heavy ovens.

It was a kitchen. A huge, airy kitchen.

"They're old," Tina said, "but last I heard, they all worked well." She opened the oven door and peered inside.

"Nice," Jess nodded, trying not to let her imagination run away with a thousand ideas for the place.

Tina leaned against the counter as Jessica's eyes roved around the room. "So, this is the thing. We need this place to pay for itself, and we need someone we can count on to run it."

Jess closed the cabinet she'd been peeking into and stood very, very still.

"And this town can use another bakery-café. A *good* bakery," she added, grimacing in the direction of the place three blocks away. "And a good baker to run it." She looked right at Jess, who couldn't quite speak. "A good businesswoman."

Jess gulped.

"So what do you say?" Tina waved her hands wide. "I was thinking the Blue Moon Saloon could use a new neighbor. Something like, I don't know...maybe the Quarter Moon Café?"

Jess struggled to say something, but nothing came out.

"Now, if you came up with a sound business plan, I'm sure we could find a way to finance it. Well?" Tina tilted her head. "What do you think?"

Jess thought she'd died and gone to heaven for the second time in two weeks.

"Um...Yes?" she squeaked. Then she hastened to add, "I have to check with my business partners, of course."

"Of course."

"And, um...um...other things..." Jess wiped her right eye before the tear building there could roll out. Her mind jumped from muffins to sandwiches to wraps. Maybe cheesecakes, too...

"Berry cheesecake?" Simon's voice came from the doorway.

Tina laughed and pressed the key into her hand. "I'll let you two think about it. You let me know when you're ready to commit."

Jess refrained from shouting *Right now!* and waved instead. "Um, sure..."

But Tina was already out the door while Simon headed in. "Sure to berry cheesecake?" His eyes twinkled.

She all but threw herself into his arms, because even a tough she-wolf could give in to her emotions from time to time. Especially when no one was looking except for her mate.

"Hey!" he protested a second later. "Why are you crying?"

"It's all so...good." So unbearably good. "Almost too good."

He hugged her tighter. "It is good."

"I mean..." She sniffed and tried to get her thoughts together. "Why do we have it so good? While Janna...and Soren..."

147

He sighed, ruffling her hair. "Janna, I reckon, is halfway to finding her mate..."

Jess knew what he meant. Janna had had her eye on Cole even before the fight, but Jess was still worried. Her sister had been unusually anxious and flighty for the past two weeks. Was Cole really the one for her? And if he was — then, damn. Female shifter-male human pairings were few and far between. She-wolves couldn't turn humans as readily as their male counterparts could. Plus, another mixed mating would give the Blue Bloods an excuse to stage yet another attack...

"And Soren..."

Jess ached just thinking about him. To have lost his mate, and so horribly, in a fire...

She held Simon even tighter. They'd had a taste of that pain. They knew how hopeless, how empty life without a mate felt.

"But maybe..."

"Maybe what?"

"Remember how I told you we dug out a den and lay down to die?"

She fisted her hands in his shirt just thinking about it. If Simon had died...

"I couldn't die for a reason. Because you were still out there," Simon said.

"You think... You think Soren's mate might still be out there? But how can that be?" When destiny brought two shifters together, they mated for life. And if one died, the other didn't simply find someone else and move on.

Simon shook his head slowly. "I don't know. Maybe he was wrong about Sarah being his mate? Maybe there's someone else?" He sighed deeply, then gathered her closer again and tucked her head under his chin. Nice and close, so that when he spoke, his voice rumbled right into her chest.

"We can't see the future, but I'd say right now is pretty damn good. And if it's good for us..."

She swallowed away the lump in her throat.

"...maybe they'll get their chance, too."

They stood there for a long time, just holding on to each other, letting the silence carry their hopes.

Then Simon leaned away from her and kissed her knuckles. "Quarter Moon Café, huh?" His eyes twinkled again, chasing away her sorrow.

"It does have a ring to it," she replied, slipping an arm around his waist. They both looked around the place.

"Dunno. All those muffins, in other people's hands..."

She laughed. "What if I promise to always reserve you a few?"

"A few?"

"Lots. As many as you like."

He made a face, but even that didn't wipe the smile out of his eyes. "God, I can see it now," he groaned. "Theme muffins."

She play-punched him in the arm and led him out to the front room. "Theme muffins. Great idea. Like mesa muffins."

"Sure. I can bite the tops off. That works for me."

"Cactus muffins..."

"Those, you can sell. Fine with me."

"They'd have pistachio glaze, dummy. To look green and lumpy on the outside, but still be tasty on the inside."

"In that case, they're mine."

She sighed and headed for the front door, jiggling the key in her hand. *Her* key, in *her* hand. Simon stopped her, though, and backed her against the wall, pressing his body against hers.

"Monsoon muffins..." She tried staying on topic as he started kissing her neck. Her neck, damn it, the one place she could never resist.

"Try again." His voice dropped an octave.

"Sunset muffins, with cherry and lemon..." Simon loved cherries almost as much as raspberries.

"Mmm," he mumbled, sucking the skin of her neck.

Her cheeks burned. Her lips twitched. Her wolf yowled.

"Um... Pinto muffins, with different flavors mixed together..."

"Not so sure," he whispered, nudging his leg between hers.

Muffins were the last thing she cared about now. Nothing mattered, not even the café. Not with her mate driving her wild all over again.

"I got it," she murmured as his hands teased her breasts.

"Yeah?"

"Hungry bear muffins." She angled her hips closer to his.

"Hungry bear," he growled. "You got that right."

"Hungry wolf, too," she threw in.

"Then I better get her to bed. Er, to the kitchen, I mean."

A lie, and she knew it. But two could play that game.

She took a deep breath and let her breasts push against his chest. Watched the color rise in his face, felt his hardness thicken in his jeans.

"Kitchen. Good idea," she mumbled. "So get to it, bear."

He threw her into a fireman's carry and headed toward the back.

"Simon!" she protested.

"Still got that key?" he rumbled.

"Yes, but..."

"Bet it works on the back door."

Her bear was a genius. They could go from the rear door of this place to the back door of the saloon, slip upstairs, and into their room.

She let her hands rove over his body as she bounced along. Being manhandled by a bear shouldn't feel this good, but what the heck. She had to live a little, right?

"You going to make love to me all over again?"

"And again and again..." he continued, all the way around the back and up the stairs. "Until forever, and then I'll start all over again."

Other books by Anna Lowe

Blue Moon Saloon

Damnation (Book 1)

Temptation (Book 2)

Redemption (Book 3)

Salvation (Book 4)

Perfection (a short story prequel to the series)

The Wolves of Twin Moon Ranch

Desert Hunt (the Prequel)

Desert Moon (Book 1)

Desert Wolf: Complete Collection (Four short stories)

Desert Blood (Book 2)

Desert Fate (Book 3)

Desert Heart (Book 4)

Desert Yule (a short story)

Desert Rose (Book 5)

Desert Roots (Book 6)

Charmed in Vegas / Shifters in Vegas

Paranormal romance with a zany twist

Gambling on Her Dragon

Gambling on Her Bear

Serendipity Adventure Romance

Off the Charts

Uncharted

Entangled

Windswept

Adrift

visit www.annalowebooks.com

Sneak Peek I: Temptation

She-wolf Janna Macks knows trouble when she sees it, especially when it comes in the form of an irresistibly brooding cowboy like Cole Harper. Her fledgling pack is already in the crosshairs of a ruthless group of rogues, and falling head over heels in lust with a human will only endanger her loved ones more. The problem is, her wolf knows her destined mate when she sees him—and Cole is it.

Rodeo pro Cole Harper has never felt this off-kilter before. One minute, he's lusting after Janna, the spunky waitress he can't get off his mind, and the next, he's growling at a dark inner voice demanding all kinds of crazy things—like howling at the moon and claiming Janna as his own. There's only one thing stronger than the overwhelming need for Janna, and that's the fear that without her, he'll succumb to the strange inner beast wrestling for control of his haunted soul.

Sneak Peek: Chapter One

Cole Harper stood before the swinging saloon doors for a good minute. Maybe two. The sun had set, and the air had that crisp, cool quality it only got in high-altitude Arizona and only on spring evenings, when everything felt fresh and budding and new.

Sounds and smells from the saloon clawed at his shoulders, begging him to come in. Laughter rang out and chairs scraped along the floor. Country music poured from the jukebox, and a couple was starting to dance. The bartender thunked down an empty glass, poured a shot of Jack Daniel's, and slid it all the way down the bar.

All that, he got without looking, just listening. Christ. What was wrong with him?

Go in, already.

Cole kept his thumbs hooked in his jeans and hunched his shoulders, trying to resist the urge.

Scents assaulted him, one after another in a thousand little punches. The peaty scent of aged whiskey, the charcoal flavor of a malt. The mouthwatering smell of spare ribs smoked over mesquite.

His tongue darted out to lick his lips before he could stop it.

Hurry up, already.

159

He'd been hearing that inner voice for a while now, and it was driving him nuts, like the itch on his arm. He'd been cut two weeks ago — a little bitty cut sustained in a fight in this very saloon, when he'd come along just in time to stop a couple of thugs from jumping the two waitresses. Unbelievably strong guys with weird, clawing nails he'd managed to avoid, except for that one scratch. His skin had healed now, but the itch remained.

An angry growl built in his throat at the memory of the intruders then faded away when he realized the sound was coming from him and not some passing dog.

Jesus, he was growling, now, too?

He coughed it away. Squaring his shoulders, he pushed the saloon's doors wide and marched in, letting them swing behind him. He took off his hat, glanced in the mirror next to the sign that read, *Check your guns at the door,* and ran his fingers through the blond hair that curled and feathered to a point somewhere beneath his ears. Then he headed straight for his chair at the end of the bar. A chair some fool was occupying, which made the growl build in his throat again.

My chair. My spot.

The inner voice was ridiculously territorial. He clenched his fists, telling himself he would not pick a fight. Telling himself it didn't matter who was sitting in which chair.

Except that fool sitting smugly in *his* chair needed to get the hell out. Now.

"Hey, Cole." A voice like honey stopped him, and his head whipped around. And just like that, the tension strung through his body like a thousand-volt current dissipated. The sights and sounds and smells of the saloon

160

faded away, and he was standing in a mountain meadow. It sure felt like that, anyway.

"Hi, Janna," he whispered.

"Hey." She smiled back.

Janna! Janna! The growl turned into a joyous inner cry.

She had her hair in two braids today, a perfect match for her bubbly, little-girl energy. Sometimes she wore it down and let it sway around her face like a liquid frame. Other times, she did this complicated braid thing he dreamed of slowly unraveling and running his fingers through. And sometimes, she just wore a ponytail, and he liked that, too.

He liked everything about Janna. A lot. Her laugh, her smile, her way of tilting her head to listen when he whispered in her ear. He'd liked her since the day he'd first set eyes on the freckled spitfire who'd started waitressing in the saloon not too long ago. Janna always had a sunny smile and sparkling eyes and a chipper voice. Her bouncy step and glossy brown hair were just as full of life as the rest of her. She had a way of looking at him as if she could see *into* him, and she didn't even seem to mind what she found.

He tightened his fingers over his belt and ordered them to stay there. Because *liking* the vivacious waitress had slid right over to *lusting* for her in the past couple of weeks. Like he'd slipped and hit some dial that turned the testosterone up full blast. All he could think of was her. Or rather, him and her. Close. Unbridled. Uncontrolled.

Which didn't make sense. He'd been there, done that with spunky cowgirl-types who could ride and rope and wrangle. What exactly did Janna have that turned on every switch in a burned-out cowboy like him?

161

Everything. She has everything. She is everything, the inner voice sighed.

When he could think straight, it scared him.

But he couldn't think straight around Janna. She was all the girls he'd ever loved, times fifty. Times a hundred. A thousand. She made him imagine all kinds of crazy things, like standing knee-deep in wildflowers in a meadow in spring. A perfect, peaceful place so unlike the reality that had been haunting him these days. The ceiling fan of the saloon that turned in lazy circles became an eagle, wheeling on a Rocky Mountain breeze. As long as Janna was around, he was in heaven.

He clenched his fists against his sides. He was in the Blue Moon Saloon, damn it. And he was not going crazy. Not yet.

"How are you doing today?" she asked, propping her drink tray against her hip.

Not crazy yet, he nearly said. *But getting closer all the time.* She was the only thing keeping him sane. In the hours he spent alone, he went through the wildest mood swings. One second, he'd be enjoying the scent of leather and horse as he saddled up a ride at the stables where he worked, and the next, he'd be overcome with the bitterest fury, the weirdest urges. Like wanting to run naked at night. Wanting to tip his chin up to the waxing moon hanging over the desert and howl at it. To chase a deer, rip into it with bare teeth, and feast on warm flesh and blood.

"Been good," he fibbed. "How about you?"

A customer walked past, and Janna stepped closer to his side.

God, she smelled nice. Like buttercups and daisies with a trace of forget-me-nots, the blue flowers that were exactly the color of her eyes. All of that blended together in a soothing scent that settled his soul.

Mine. Mate.

He shook his head and looked around, hoping to spot some guy hiding somewhere, throwing his voice. But there was no one. Just the dark, husky voice in his mind that he didn't trust one bit. What was with the mate nonsense, anyway?

"Happy to see you." Janna smiled and tilted forward on the balls of her feet. Just enough that if he wanted, he could kiss her.

It wouldn't be their first kiss, either, because they'd been out dancing a few weeks back, before he'd started losing his mind. It was the first night he'd enjoyed in a long, long time. A great night, even, breathing her in and holding her close and only letting go long enough to whirl her around then pull her straight back into his arms, where he'd whispered in her ear and made her laugh and smile that incredible smile. Fast dancing turned into slow dancing, and slow dancing turned into a melting kind of grind, and the kiss was only the first of many he had planned to shower on her all the way back to his place.

But her friends had interrupted them, and though she'd all but snarled them off, he'd come to his senses and backed away for her own good. He could get drunk on Janna, but she deserved better than him.

Kiss her, the voice growled. *Take her. Mark her!*

He took half a step back. That voice was dangerous. Demanding. Crude. A man didn't *take* from a woman. Not the kind of man he'd been raised to be.

Believe me, she's asking, the voice shot back.

Well, if she was, he had to be the one who kept a clear head. So what if their bodies breezed into a crazy high

163

just from being close?

Need her to survive the Change, the voice inside him murmured. *Need my mate.*

He shivered. Survive? Change? Mate? He truly was losing his mind.

Being around Janna slowed it down, though. She calmed him down. Well, most of the time. Usually, she made him think of a place like that idyllic meadow, where he could lie down with his head in her lap and settle into a profound peace. Sometimes, though, all he could imagine was rolling with her in that meadow. Stripping off her clothes and his and pounding inside her as she wrapped her legs around him and raked her nails across his back. He'd imagine pumping his hips as madly as she'd pump hers while she screamed her pleasure and—

"You okay?" Her brow furrowed.

He took a deep breath and winced at the crushing hardness in his jeans. "Good. Yeah. Great." A lie, but it was better than the truth. *Not okay. Thinking of throwing you over my shoulder and fucking you nowhere near as gently as you deserve.*

Her nostrils flared, and for the briefest of instants, he wondered if she'd like that.

He turned to the bar, trying to clear his mind — only to spot the asshole sitting in his chair again. *His* chair!

He clenched his teeth and his fists, because anger came with an awful, pinching pain under his nails and canines, like they were being pulled out by pliers. Or worse, pushed out from inside to make space for—

"Cole," Janna murmured. The second she put a hand on his arm, the pain faded along with the fury. "I got this."

164

She scurried ahead and smiled at the man while Cole glared from over her shoulder. Janna was tall, only a couple of inches under his six feet, and she had a self-assured poise that doubled her presence.

"We've got a table for you now," she told the customer, pointing.

Cole gritted his teeth and told himself she was smiling at the guy because it was her job, not because the ass deserved it.

"Thanks, sitting at the bar is fine." The man's smile was aimed at Janna, but when his gaze turned to Cole, it faded fast. "On second thought..." He grabbed his drink and fled.

Cole glared at the man's back until Janna stuck an elbow in his ribs, squelching the growl he wasn't aware of until then.

"Look." She patted the barstool and made her voice silky-sweet. "All yours."

Her hand ran over his shoulder, and their eyes met.

All mine, the voice hummed inside.

"All yours." She nodded.

His eyes went wide. Did she really mean...

She steered him onto the stool, and her hands on his waist felt good. Like dancing had been — that feeling of rightness, of belonging, of a perfect fit.

He sat down and she came a little closer. Closer still, like she was getting sucked into the magic spell, too. It took everything he had not to pull her into the space between his legs and deliver a huge, bruising kiss.

"Janna!" the big guy working the bar called. Simon Voss, one of two brothers who ran the place. Well, they pretended to run the place. It was Janna and her sister, the waitresses, who made the place thrive. The brothers

165

were good at security, though, and kept the customers on their best behavior when it came to Janna and Jessica. And Cole was a regular, so they were okay with him, not to mention grateful for his intervention that night of the attack.

Still, Simon shot him a look that said, *Watch it, cowboy. Got my eye on you, too.*

Cole wanted to protest. *Hey, you can trust me!* But he couldn't even trust himself these days, so why should Simon?

Janna pulled away, and his heart ached just at that much space opening up between them. Then she ran a smooth palm over his cheek and whispered, "Be right back," making his soul settle again.

"I'll be right here," he growled as she went. It was a promise and a warning to anyone eyeing her perfect ass. And there were plenty of suspects on that count. A whole saloon full of them, it felt like.

And jeez, the place was hopping tonight. Before Janna and her sister came along, the saloon hadn't pulled in half as many customers. It was listless and dusty and dead — sort of the way he felt. But then Janna had filled it with laughter and smiles and life, and he started coming because... because...

Well, maybe in spite of himself.

Janna shot him one parting smile over her shoulder, making him go warm all over.

Mine, the inner voice growled. *Mate.*

"I'll be right here," he whispered. "I'll be right here."

Get you copy of *Temptation* today!

About the Author

USA Today and Amazon bestselling author Anna Lowe loves putting the "hero" back into heroine and letting location ignite a passionate romance. She likes a heroine who is independent, intelligent, and imperfect – a woman who is doing just fine on her own. But give the heroine a good man – not to mention a chance to overcome her own inhibitions – and she'll never turn down the chance for adventure, nor shy away from danger.

Anna loves dogs, sports, and travel – and letting those inspire her fiction. On any given weekend, you might find her hiking in the mountains or hunched over her laptop, working on her latest story. Either way, the day will end with a chunk of dark chocolate and a good read.

Visit *AnnaLoweBooks.com*

Made in the USA
Coppell, TX
02 May 2022